Michelle Smart's love affair with books started when she was a baby and would cuddle them in her cot. A voracious reader of all genres, she found her love of romance established when she stumbled across her first Mills & Boon book at the age of twelve. She's been reading them—and writing them—ever since. Michelle lives in Northamptonshire, England, with her husband and two young Smarties.

BILLIONAIRE'S BABY OF REDEMPTION

MICHELLE SMART

MILLS & BOON

First Published in Great Britain 2018
by Mills & Boon, an imprint of HarperCollins*Publishers*
1 London Bridge Street, London, SE1 9GF

© 2018 Michelle Smart

ISBN: 978-0-263-93484-7

MIX
Paper from
responsible sources

FSC www.fsc.org   **FSC** C007454

Printed and bound in Spain
by CPI, Barcelona

This book is for Jennifer Hayward, Pippa Roscoe and Nic Caws, who all made the writing of Javier and Sophie's story an utter joy. xxx

CHAPTER ONE

JAVIER CASILLAS KEPT his eyes fixed on the wide corridor ahead of him, jaw clenched, feet working automatically. He could feel the eyes upon him; had felt them all evening in the private box he shared with his twin. He'd steeled himself for it. His wildly infamous parentage meant the media spotlight was something he'd learned to endure but the past two months had magnified that spotlight by a thousand.

He would give them exactly what he had always given them. Nothing.

He had not allowed a flicker of emotion to pass his face throughout the performance.

Inside, the rage had built. He'd watched Freya, the woman he'd intended to marry, put on the performance of her life, listened to the rapturous applause, and all he had wanted to do was go home and beat the hell out of his punching bag.

Tonight was the culmination of a long-standing dream between Javier and his twin brother, Luis. A decade ago they'd finally had the funds to purchase the crumbling Madrid theatre and ballet school their prima ballerina mother had spent her childhood learning to dance at, buying the ballet company with it. They'd renamed it Compania de Ballet de Casillas in her memory and set about turning it into one of the most eminent ballet companies in Europe. They'd then bought another parcel of land close to it and built on it a brand-new state-of-the-art theatre and ballet school. Tonight was its grand opening. The world's media was out in force, but instead of focussing on the theatre and ballet company and celebrating Clara Casillas's memory, their focus was on Javier and his ex-fiancée.

The whole damn world knew she'd left him for his oldest friend.

What the whole world did not yet know was that Benjamin Guillem had stolen her in a sick game of revenge and that Freya had been happy to be stolen.

They were welcome to each other. Freya meant nothing to Javier. She never had.

The corridor he walked through on his way to the aftershow party forked. About to turn left with the group he was with, which included members of the Spanish royal family, Javier felt a hand settle on his shoulder and steer him firmly in the other direction.

No one other than his twin would have dared touch him in such a manner.

'What's the matter?' Javier asked, staring at his brother with suspicion as they walked.

'I wanted to talk to you alone,' Luis replied.

There was something in his brother's tone that lifted the hairs on the nape of his neck.

Tension had simmered between them since his twin's foolhardy trip to the Caribbean. How Luis thought that marrying Benjamin's sister would restore their reputations was still, well over a month on, beyond Javier's comprehension. Although wildly different from him in both looks and personality, his brother usually had excellent judgement. His opinion was the only one Javier ever thought worthy of consideration.

Fortunately his brother had seen sense at the last minute and returned to Madrid as a single man but things had not been right between them since.

Luis was his only constant. It had been the two of them, facing the world and everything it could throw at them, together, since they had shared the same womb.

Luis waited until they were out of anyone's earshot before turning to him. 'You knew we were ripping Benjamin off all those years ago, didn't you?'

The rage that had simmered in Javier all evening blazed at the mention of his nemesis's name.

Seven years ago the Casillas brothers had invited Benjamin to invest in a project they were undertaking in Paris, the creation of a skyscraper that became known as Tour Mont Blanc. They had invited his investment only because the seller of the land, to whom they had paid a significant deposit, suddenly told them they had until midnight to pay the balance or he would sell to another interested buyer. They didn't have the cash. Benjamin did.

'We didn't rip him off,' Javier reminded him icily. 'He was the fool who signed the contract without reading it.'

'And you should have warned him the terms had changed as you'd said you would. You didn't forget, did you?'

Javier might be many things but a liar was not one of them.

Luis had been the one to invite Benjamin onto the project. His investment was worth twenty per cent of the land fee. In the rush of sealing the deal Luis had told Benjamin it meant twenty per cent of the profits. Their lawyer, who drew up the contract in record time, had been the one to point out that the Casillas brothers would be doing all the work and that Benjamin's profit share should be only five per cent, a point Javier had agreed with.

The contract had been changed accordingly. Javier had emailed it to Benjamin expecting him to read the damn thing and negotiate if the new terms were not to his liking.

'I knew it.' Luis took a deep breath. 'All these years

and I've told myself that it had been an oversight on your part when I should have accepted the truth that you never forget. In thirty-five years you have never forgotten anything or failed to do something you promised.'

'I never promised to email him.' Javier never made promises he didn't intend to keep. People could say what they liked about him—and frequently did, although never to his face—but he was a man of his word.

'Not an actual promise,' Luis conceded. 'But look me in the eye and tell me it wasn't a deliberate act on your part.'

Luis had asked him to give Benjamin a heads-up about the changes in terms when Javier emailed the contract. At no point had Javier agreed to this request and Luis should be thankful for it. Benjamin's failure to read the contract before signing it had made the Casillas brothers richer to the tune of two hundred and twenty-five million euros. Benjamin had still made an excellent profit—*profit*—of seventy-five million and all he'd had to do for that substantial sum was transfer some funds. That he'd had the nerve to sue them over it was beyond the pale. That Benjamin had refused to accept the court's judgement when the judge had thrown the case out, and then stolen Javier's fiancée from him, was despicable.

And the world thought *he* was the bad man in all this?

Blind, prejudiced fools, the lot of them. He knew what they all thought. The world looked at his face and saw his murderer father.

'For what reason would it have been deliberate?' he asked coldly.

'That is for your conscience to decide. All I know for sure is that Benjamin was our friend. I have defended you and I have fought your corner—'

'*Our* corner,' Javier corrected, his limited patience right at the point of snapping.

Now his own *twin* was questioning his motives?

What happened to the loyalty that had always bound them together?

'I assume this burst of conscience from you is connected to that damned woman.'

He'd had a sense of foreboding in the pit of his stomach since spotting Chloe Guillem, Benjamin's sister, in the audience that night.

Chloe had betrayed them as greatly as her brother had; had aided and abetted his plot to steal Freya and was, unquestionably, the cause of all the tension that had hung between Javier and Luis since Luis's return from the Caribbean.

A darkness rarely seen on his brother's face suddenly appeared, and before Javier had time to blink, Luis had grabbed him by the collar of his shirt. 'If you ever speak about Chloe in that way again then you and I are finished. Do you hear me? Finished.'

'If you're still defending her to me then I would say we're already finished, *brother*.' He spat the last word directly into Luis's face.

Javier knew in his bones that something had happened between Luis and Chloe. Luis had always had a roving eye for the ladies but never had Javier had cause to suspect a shift in his brother's loyalty from it.

If Luis wanted to be with that bitch after what she had done to him then Luis could get the hell out of his life. Loyalty counted for everything and if Luis had lost sight of that then he was no brother to him.

Eyeball to eyeball, they glowered at each other, the venom seeping between them thick enough to taste.

Then Luis released his hold and stepped back.

Javier stared at the man he had shared a womb with, had shared a bedroom with, had fought with, had protected, had been protected by, had grieved with, the other side of the coin that was the Casillas twins, and watched him take backwards strides until he turned his back on him.

Breathing heavily, his hands clenched into fists, his hardening heart thumping, Javier watched Luis collide with a petite blonde woman in his haste to get away from him.

In all their thirty-five years neither of them had ever turned their back on the other.

It would be the first and last time Luis walked away from him.

In the periphery of his vision he saw the woman his treacherous brother had bumped into come towards him, but with his gaze on Luis's retreating back, it was only when she stood a few feet from him that her features came into focus.

Javier stared at the face he had last seen two months before when he had shown her to the door of his house.

Big pale blue eyes stared back, apprehension shining out of them.

The rage inside him ratcheted up another notch. Any higher and there was real danger he would combust.

This was a face he had never wanted to see close-up again.

'You should be at the aftershow party,' he snapped.

Sophie Johnson was part of Compania de Ballet de Casillas's *corps de ballet* and had a contractual obligation to attend the aftershow party.

Colour flamed the pretty heart-shaped face, a pained crease forming in her brow. 'I quit the company two months ago.'

His heart thumped to hear that surprisingly sultry voice again.

Sophie had the sweet looks of an innocent but a voice that evoked thoughts of dark red satin sheets and dim lighting.

She had quit the company…?

He had hardly looked at the stage during the performance.

'Then what the hell are you doing here?'

But he knew. The pressing weight in his already tightly crushed chest told him the answer. He did not want to listen to it.

Her throat moved.

He'd kissed that throat…

'I need to talk to you.'

'Now is the worst time to speak to me.' And she was the last person he wished to see or speak to. Not now, when he could feel the fabric of his life dissolving around him.

He stepped past her and nodded a dismissal. 'Excuse me.'

He'd taken no more than two paces when she said, 'It's important.'

His heart began to thrum wildly, every nerve ending standing on edge. Memories of their brief interlude surfaced in a wave, memories he'd not allowed himself to think of since showing her out of his home.

Pinching the bridge of his nose, he half turned to her and inhaled deeply.

'No,' he told her harshly. 'This is not a conversation we are going to have now. Go home.'

'But—'

'I said *no*.'

The vehemence in Javier's gravelly tone made Sophie recoil.

She watched him stride down the long corridor, clenching her jaw so tightly it stopped the threatening tears from splashing over her cheeks.

She had shed enough tears these past two months.

She staggered on shaking legs to the nearest chair and sank down into it.

Covering her mouth, she forced deep breaths into her choking airway and drew on all the ballet training that had been instilled in her since early childhood to stop her frame collapsing.

A glamorous couple strolled past her, hand in hand, the woman giving Sophie a sideways glance.

She tried to give the smile that normally came automatically whenever she met another person's eye but could barely move her cheek muscles.

She had once thought herself in love with Javier. *Fool!*

The stories about him being a cold-hearted bastard had all proven themselves to be true.

That she had ignored them, convinced that his was a soul in torment and that his reputation was not formed from a heart set in stone, was her own fault.

Sophie had taken one look at Javier when he'd paid a visit to the ballet company almost a year ago and felt her heart move and all the breath leave her body in a rush.

It had been a visceral reaction unlike anything she had experienced before.

Unlike the sculpted men of the ballet world, Javier was a bone crusher of a man, enormously tall and broad with a presence that made everyone look twice. He wasn't handsome in the traditional sense, his nose too wide and with a bend to it, his light brown eyes too hooded and with a permanent look of suspicion etched in them to ever be considered a pin-up, but he had a magnetism that turned those flaws into something mesmerising. He had mesmerised her in more ways than one. Always attuned to others' emotions, the pain she had sensed in Javier had reached deep into her.

She had spent months longing for a glimpse of him. The times she did—and they were rare times, his involvement with the day-to-day running of the ballet company minimal—her heart would soar. She had known it was a crush that would go nowhere. Javier Casillas was the co-owner of her ballet company, a property magnate with a net worth she could scarcely comprehend, an arrogant, aloof figure who conjured fear and admiration in equal measure. He would never look twice at her.

But he did look twice at Freya.

Freya was her oldest and closest friend, the reason for Sophie being in Madrid dancing for the company that had made Freya a star. Freya was beautiful. Freya was a dancer with the world at her pointe shoes, a dancer who stole the heart of everyone who watched her perform.

Sophie had never shared her feelings for Javier with Freya. It had been too personal and unlikely to share with anyone.

Javier's marriage proposal and Freya's acceptance of it had devastated her.

For months she had sat on her despondency, determined to support her oldest friend even if she did have grave misgivings about their forthcoming loveless marriage that had nothing to do with her own breaking heart. She even gamely agreed to be their bridesmaid.

Then, the week before they were due to exchange their vows, Freya had run off with Benjamin Guillem, leaving Javier for dust. A media frenzy had ensued.

Sophie had been trying to do a good deed when she'd gone to Javier's home. She'd been packing Freya's stuff for her from the flat they shared and had come across a copy of Freya and Javier's prenuptial agreement and a file of other pertinent legal documents. Freya didn't want them, so, not knowing what else to do, Sophie had decided the best thing would be to let Javier decide. She was pretty sure he wouldn't want the documents to reach the public domain.

The day after Freya and Benjamin married, Sophie had braced herself and set off for Javier's home.

His house was a secluded villa that more resembled a

palace than a home. She'd had to speak into a camera before the electric gates had slowly opened and admitted her into his domain.

She remembered walking the long driveway, sick to her stomach with pain for him. He might not have loved Freya but he must be shattered that she had left him for his oldest friend and in such a public fashion too.

The whole world knew about it and had put the blame squarely on Javier's shoulders without knowing even a basic fact—even she didn't know a fact about it, Freya's only communication being the one asking her to pack her belongings together—and was seeming to revel in portraying him as a monster in disguise. Sophie's heart had twisted to hear the vile rumours about him.

Expecting a member of his household staff to open the front door for her, she had been surprised to find it opened by Javier himself.

What followed had been even more unexpected.

That was when she'd understood his ruthless reputation had been based on truth.

If he'd even given her a single thought since, he would have known she'd left his ballet company, left Madrid and returned to England. In the vain hope he would seek her out she had left her forwarding address on the company files. He could have found her without any effort if he had wanted to.

He hadn't even noticed her absence from the stage that night.

She'd used those two months of silence to come to terms with the reality of her situation and get herself in an emotional place where she could face Javier again.

She would seek him out again tomorrow; seek him every single day until he was willing to have the conversation they so desperately needed to have.

Only when she was certain she could get back to her

feet without her legs crumpling did she stand up, inhaling deeply.

Concentrating on putting one foot in front of the other, Sophie headed back the way she had come. The theatre's wide corridors were almost deserted now.

When she reached the top of the ornate red-carpeted stairs that led down into the foyer, her heart skipped to see Javier striding up to her, his long legs taking the steps two at a time.

She held tightly onto the gold railing and stared at the emotionless, menacing face fixed on her.

When he reached the top, he inclined his head for her to follow him, leading her to a secluded section of the corridor.

He stopped walking and gazed down at her, breathing heavily through his nose.

'Why now?' He ran a hand through his hair. 'Why did you choose tonight of all nights to tell me? Why not approach me in private?'

She kept her gaze steady on him. 'Because after the way you treated me, I didn't trust you would agree to see or speak to me.'

He had gone from blazing passion to ice-cold in the whisper of a second.

He had escorted her out of his home.

His face twisted. 'You are carrying my child?'

How she kept her composure to answer him without bursting into tears she would never know. 'Yes. We're going to have a baby.'

CHAPTER TWO

HOT DARKNESS FILLED Javier's head, swimming like a blood-red fog through him.

He'd known the moment Sophie had come into focus why she was there but his already overwhelmed brain had fought to deny it.

He was going to be a father.

But the mother wasn't the perfect woman he had sought to bear his children but this waif-like creature who had ignited something in him that should never have been allowed to breathe.

He wanted children. He and his treacherous brother had adopted their mother's surname the moment they could legally dump their father's and he wanted to carry that name on to the next generation.

He'd waited his entire adult life for the perfect woman to come along and bear him those children.

Freya had been that woman. Beautiful, coldly perfect Freya, who would have given him beautiful, perfect children and who had not elicited the smallest glimmer of desire in him and shown no desire for him either. Perfection in all ways.

Javier knew the danger of passion. His orphaned state was living proof of those dangers.

The dangerous blood that had swirled in his father lived in his own veins too. It pumped hot and strong inside him, a living thing he was reminded of every time he looked in a mirror.

He should never have allowed Sophie, this warm-blooded, sensitive creature, to come anywhere within his orbit.

She sighed and pulled a business card from the small black bag she carried. She held it out to him with those tiny fingers that had caused such mayhem to his skin when she had touched him.

'This is the hotel I'm staying at,' she said quietly. 'Take the time to process what's happening and then come and find me when you're ready to talk.'

'What is there to talk about?' he asked roughly, not taking the card, not willing to risk touching her in any way.

He knew what he had to do. There was no point in wasting air discussing what was a foregone conclusion.

He'd walked away from her with his head reeling and the weight of the world crashing down on him. He'd intended to work all the stress out and bring himself to a point where he could trust himself to have this difficult conversation without exploding.

He'd got as far as his car when the implications had really hit him and he'd known that to leave her there would make him as big a monster as the world believed him to be.

'We're having a baby, Javier. I would say there's a lot to talk about.'

'Not for me there isn't. If you're carrying my child then there's only one thing that needs to be decided on and that's the date of our wedding.'

She blinked. 'You are willing to marry me?'

'My child will bear my name and if you want any kind of financial support from me then you will agree to it.'

Sophie was naïve. Damn her, she'd been a virgin, a fact she had neglected to mention when they'd been ripping each other's clothes off.

If she had any illusions about him or their future relationship let her have them dispelled now. If she didn't already know what kind of a man he was—and his failure to seek her out in any form these past few months must have given her some clue—then let her know now.

She would never know it but he was doing her a kindness.

To his surprise, a small smile curved her pretty lips. 'You don't have to threaten me. I want us to marry.'

That took him aback. 'You do?'

Her throat moved as she nodded.

He laughed, a guttural sound that grated to his own ears. For all her naivety and surface sweetness, Sophie was already making the financial calculations of how being his wife would significantly improve her bank account.

But there was no returning laugh from Sophie. Her eyes did not flicker or leave his face. 'Our child is innocent. It did not choose to be conceived. It deserves to know and be wanted by both its parents.'

He made no attempt to hide his cynicism. 'If that is true then why wait so long to tell me? You must have known for weeks.'

He was no pregnancy expert but he had studied biology at school and knew the ways a woman's body worked.

'I knew within a week,' she said steadily. 'I could feel changes happening inside me. I took the test the day after my period was due, so I have known for certain for six weeks. Technically I'm ten weeks pregnant as the due date is taken from the date of my last period. I waited before telling you because I needed my head to be in the right place before I faced you again.'

'Did you have to research the best ways to leverage cash from the situation?' he mocked brutally. He had never met a woman who didn't have cash signs ringing in her eyes.

Having more money than he could spend in a thousand

lifetimes was good for many things but leverage was its greatest gift. He'd used his wealth to buy Freya and she, the coldly perfect prima ballerina that she was, had been happy to be purchased. It was what had made her so ideal for him. 'Is that why you have set your path on marriage to me?'

But, again, there was no flicker in Sophie's pale blue eyes. 'I want nothing but what is best for our child.'

From the corner of his eye he saw two security guards approach. They would be making a sweep of the theatre before locking up for the night; the aftershow party taking place in a basement conference room.

If there was one thing Javier despised it was people knowing his business. His family had been fodder for the world's consumption since before his birth.

He might still be trying to process that he was going to be a father but already he knew that he would do whatever it took to protect his child.

Rubbing his jaw, he took a deep breath. 'Whatever you say your motives are, our unborn child is the only thing that matters.'

'Yes,' she interjected softly.

'It is late. This is something that needs to be discussed when we have fresh minds. I have had an incredibly difficult day.' She couldn't begin to understand how difficult it had been. 'My driver will take you to your hotel. Get some sleep. You look tired.'

That made her eyes flicker.

'I'll have you brought to me in the morning,' he continued, now walking back to the stairs. He kept his eyes focussed straight ahead of him, no longer wishing to look at the woman who had just detonated a bomb into his already turbulent life.

The bomb was of his own making, he accepted grimly.

He was the damn fool who had failed to use a condom for the first and only time in his life.

He was the fool who'd invited her into his home.

Their baby was the consequence of that foolhardiness and, as Sophie had already pointed out, an innocent in all of this.

She remained silent as she kept pace beside him, silent all the way down the stairs and through the foyer. Only when they reached the exit door did she turn to him and say, 'What time will your driver collect me in the morning?'

'Arrange that with him.' He stepped out into the warm night air and strode to his waiting driver.

'Take Miss Johnson to her hotel,' he said, then, without a word of goodbye or a second glance at her, set off for his home.

He could feel Sophie's gaze upon him but kept his sight fixed ahead, increasing his pace.

As he power-walked the three miles to his home, the memories he'd spent two months suppressing came back to him with crystal clarity.

He'd woken that fateful day to the news Freya and Benjamin had married and a barrage of hate mail. Someone had leaked his personal email address online and keyboard warriors had had an excellent time aiming their poisoned ire at him. So angry had he been that he'd dismissed his household staff for the day.

His rage was best kept private. It was safer that way. For everyone.

And then his intercom had rung and he'd looked through the monitor to see Sophie standing there, a thick folder in her arms, which, she had claimed over the intercom, contained private documents of his.

He'd recognised her immediately. Freya's dance colleague and flatmate. The wallflower who had never met his eye on the few occasions he'd been in her presence. If anyone had inside information on Freya and Benjamin's treachery that he could use to his advantage it would be her.

It had been a baking summer's day. She'd been dressed in a thin pale grey shirt dress, her long light blonde hair tied in a loose plait. When she'd removed enormous sunglasses to speak to him and fixed huge pale blue eyes on him, he'd seen compassion shining from them.

Not once in his adult life had he stared anyone in the eye and not seen a glimmer of fear shine back at him. Grown men, titans of industry and power brokers would shake his hand with a nervous laugh; glamorous, self-confident women would give him the come-to-bed eyes with excitement-laced fear.

This young English woman, a petite ballerina with the appearance of a waif, had turned up at his home and displayed not an ounce of fright.

The rage that had been bubbling so furiously inside him had suddenly reduced.

She had given him the sweetest, most sympathetic smile he'd ever been on the receiving end of. 'How are you holding up?' she'd asked softly.

In the week since Benjamin had stolen Freya from him, Sophie was the first person to have asked him that. The most he'd received from his twin had been a stoical slap to the shoulder.

He'd invited her in, made her a coffee, led her to the dining room, sat beside her at the huge table with the documents between them and quizzed her.

When she'd professed her innocence in the matter of Freya and Benjamin, he'd been surprised to find he believed her.

This belief had disconcerted him.

She had disconcerted him with those non-judgemental eyes and her subtle yet obvious compassion.

He'd found himself trying to get a rise out of her, asking if she'd read the documents, making it sound like an accusation.

She'd been unfazed and unabashed. She'd nodded and said, 'Yes, I read through them with Freya. I won't be sharing them with anyone, so don't worry.'

'You won't share the details with the media?' he'd asked cynically.

'If I wanted to share anything with them I would have done so by now. They've been camped outside my apartment block all week.'

Something had crept into his veins at that, something he'd never felt before.

That this petite young thing should be harassed with no one there to protect her had set the anger boiling again.

Of course, he knew her waif-like frame belied a physical strength all ballerinas had but that didn't change what his eyes saw when he looked at her.

Dios, he'd been unable to tear his eyes from her. He had never seen such naturally pink rosebud lips before…

A new kind of tension had sparked to life.

Sophie's eyes had kept flickering to him, then darting away, pretty colour flushing across her pretty cheeks.

She really was incredibly pretty. How had he not noticed it before…?

He'd found himself leaning closer to her, catching a whiff of a light, floral perfume that had delighted his senses.

'Speaking with the media would boost your profile,' he'd pointed out.

A burst of antipathy had glittered in her eyes. 'I don't care. I'm not going to add to the frenzy and make things worse for you.'

Again, he'd found himself believing her but also curious...
Worse for *him*?

She didn't even know him.

Professional dancers spent their lives fighting to get to the top and when you were as driven as that any advantage for name recognition would be snatched upon. His own mother had been shameless in her quest for media attention.

Sophie had ducked her head and refused to answer questions even when it would have seen her face plastered over the tabloids as a bit player in the biggest scandal Spain—indeed, most of Europe—had had for years.

What was her agenda? Everyone had one, so what was hers? Why go out of her way for him?

He'd leaned even closer and dropped his voice to a murmur. 'Why are you here?'

The colour already staining her cheeks had darkened, the pale blue eyes darkening with it. It had been the most beguiling sight.

She had cleared her throat, the pink rosebud lips opening and closing as if she were trying to get out words that did not want to be revealed.

It was sheer impulse that had led him to kiss those lips.

What happened next had been utter madness.

Javier increased his pace and inhaled the Madrid autumn night air deeply to counteract the blood thickening all over again at the vivid memories.

She had kissed him back.

And then he had hauled her out of her chair and into his arms.

For a few brief moments all his torment and anger had been dispelled and forgotten.

Sophie's kisses had been the sweetest he had ever tasted and instantly addictive.

Desire like nothing he had ever experienced had pulsed through him. Heady, hungry and utterly consuming.

He tried to throw the memories off him now, not wanting to remember any more, disgusted with himself for the manner in which he'd used her hot, willing body.

That was his only saving grace, he thought grimly.

Sophie had been utterly willing.

There had been nothing one-sided about it.

In that moment, the madness had lived in both of them.

He'd spread her flat on his dining table, drinking in her hot, sweet kisses as he'd plunged into her that first time. He'd felt the resistance of her body and known in an instant what it had meant.

Her eyes had widened.

He would have pulled out there and then if she hadn't then smiled at him, put her hands to his face and kissed him so deeply that he had lost all sense of himself.

But as soon as it was over the only thing he'd been able to taste was revulsion, at himself for his actions and at Sophie for throwing away her virginity in such a seedy way and on a man such as him.

But mostly at himself.

They hadn't used any protection.

He hadn't used any protection.

He'd needed her gone before he said or did something he regretted.

He felt no pride in remembering how he'd coldly walked to his front door and held it open for her.

She would never know it but he'd been saving her from herself.

And now she was pregnant. Sweet, sweet Sophie was pregnant with his child.

Damn it all to hell.

Javier had experienced only one day worse than this. The day his father had murdered his mother.

* * *

Sophie waited until the driver opened her door before stepping out in front of the imposing Tuscan-style villa that was Javier's home.

The first time she had been there she had been filled with so many emotions she had hardly taken anything in other than its titanic size.

Now there was an array of sights and smells filling her senses. She'd noticed that increase in her perceptions during the first week of her pregnancy. It was like discovering secrets of the world, an unexpected symptom that warmed her.

She needed all the warmth she could get.

She'd lain in her hotel bed telling herself over and over that she was doing the right thing. Not telling Javier about the pregnancy had never been on the cards. He was the father. He deserved to know and deserved to be involved if that was what he wanted.

She was glad for their child's sake that he did want to be and that he'd come to the decision of marriage so quickly. For once, it hadn't been the anguish she always felt at the thought of disappointing her adoptive parents, good, loving, decent people who believed strongly in the sanctity of marriage, but for her child. Her child deserved nothing less.

Sophie often thought of her biological father. Had he ever known of her conception? Had he been party to the decision to abandon her? Or had he spent twenty-four years unaware he had a daughter out there, being raised by people who were strangers to him?

These were just some of the many questions that had haunted her life. She had long stopped seeking answers for them—they all led to dead ends—but had never stopped wondering. She would wonder about the man and woman who had given her life for ever.

Her child would not. Whatever happened between Sophie and Javier, her child would know who both its parents were.

Stepping onto the marble stairs that led to a wraparound porch, Sophie followed the driver, who had insisted on taking her suitcase, to the front door.

Everything about Javier's home looked so much richer and more palatial than her first and last visit. Private and secluded from the bustle of Madrid's busy streets, it screamed opulence. This was the kind of house any self-regarding billionaire would be proud to call home.

Marble pillars flagged the wide oak door that opened before the driver could raise his hand to knock.

Javier stood there, casually dressed in an olive-green shirt unbuttoned at the neck and black jeans that showcased the muscularity of his thighs. Thick stubble covered his jawline. His hooded light brown eyes met hers for the briefest of moments before he nodded his thanks at the driver and dismissed him.

'Refreshments are being made for us,' he said as he led her through the grand reception room twice as high as a normal room and adorned with ancient Egyptian relics, including a bust of a sphinx almost as large as Javier himself.

The first time she had been there she had been too overawed at being invited in by the man she had mooned over for so long to pay much attention to anything, but now she was determined to keep an analytical head and pay attention to everything.

'Is it okay to leave my suitcase in here?' she asked.

He stopped and turned, a frown creasing his forehead, fleshy, sensuous lips pulling together. 'Why have you brought your suitcase with you?'

'I checked out of my hotel.'

Now his eyes narrowed. 'I hope you are not expecting to move in today.'

'I've checked out of the hotel because my reason for staying in it is done—you know about the baby. I'll fly back to England when we've finished discussing everything and set a game plan out.'

Disconcerted, Javier ran his fingers through his hair. He could read nothing but honesty in Sophie's wide gaze and he didn't trust it an inch.

The dreamless sleep he had hoped for had proven fruitless. He doubted he'd had more than an hour of solid sleep.

Sophie was pregnant with his child. The puffiness of her eyes was proof she must have found sleep as elusive as he had, but where his stomach was knotted with thorny barbs she had a calm serenity about her.

She'd had a head start on getting her head around being a parent, he reminded himself grimly. She'd known for certain for six whole weeks and had kept it to herself when she should have told him immediately.

Dios, his head felt ready to combust. All these betrayals, it was like a sickness. Benjamin's refusal to accept his own negligence and then stealing Freya from him had been only the start, culminating in the disaster that had been the night before, the night when he and his twin celebrated their mother's memory with a world determined to remember her torrid death rather than her magnificent life, now tainted for ever. Luis, his own twin, had betrayed it and had betrayed him so greatly it felt as if he'd been sucker-punched. The business they had built from nothing would have to be split, the brotherhood that had driven his life rent apart with one gross act of disloyalty.

And he was going to be a father. He was going to marry a woman so far removed from his ideal of what a suitable wife for himself should be that she could be from Venus.

'Let us discuss our game plan now,' he said icily, leading her through to one of his four living rooms, his least favourite for relaxing. He would never allow himself to relax again around Sophie. It was too dangerous, especially for her.

Initially he'd planned for their meeting to take place in the dining room but when he'd stepped into it a powerful memory of making love to her on that table had sent a thrill of desire racing through him, so, with a click of his fingers, he'd ordered the documents to be moved.

He indicated the sofas arranged in a square around a coffee table. 'Take a seat.'

She obeyed his command by sitting gracefully and crossing her legs.

He wished she hadn't. Until that moment he had refused to pay any attention to her attire but now his eyes focussed on the athletic but decidedly feminine figure clad in fashionably ripped jeans and an oversized thin sweater that fell off the shoulder. She'd left her long blonde hair loose.

A member of his staff entered the room carrying the refreshments he'd ordered and he was glad of the diversion.

He waited until the drinks and pastries had been laid out before seating himself opposite Sophie and pouring himself a coffee. 'Help yourself.'

Again, she obeyed. Soon she had a palmier on a plate on her lap and was sipping a glass of fresh orange juice.

He allowed himself a slight breath of relief. So far she was displaying all the signs of obedience. Things would be much easier if she were to fall in with his plans without questioning them. He knew little about Sophie but the impression he'd formed before he'd stupidly made love to her had been of a shy woman who had little in the way of spine or gumption.

He'd climbed out of his bed that morning knowing he needed to learn something concrete about the woman he was going to marry, so he had woken the ballet company's human resources manager, ordering her to email Sophie's employment file to him. It had been a quick but illuminating read. Sophie had been educated at the same ballet school as Freya, worked for a provincial English ballet company upon her graduation, then followed Freya to Madrid. She'd had no starring roles in any ballet production of note and was described in the file as warm but shy.

It had been illuminating in that it had confirmed his prior thoughts about her.

She was probably so relieved he'd agreed to marry her that she would now agree to anything to keep him onside.

Perfect.

He downed his black coffee and poured another, then waited until she had bitten a delicate amount of pastry before saying, 'Those documents on the table are for you to read through. They're the prenuptial agreement you'll need to sign before we can marry.'

Her eyes remained on his face as she chewed slowly. When she swallowed, a flicker of pink tongue popped to the side of her mouth to lick a stray crumb.

Javier inhaled deeply and forced his attention back to the documents she now leaned forward to pick up, only to be confronted by a glimpse of cleavage as her sweater dipped.

He clenched his hands into fists and commanded his loins to stay neutral.

Sophie was only a woman. There was nothing special about her, nothing that should make his loins twitch and his veins heat. He would not allow the memories of their one time together to trick his body.

She leaned back and casually flicked through the documents he'd woken his lawyer at six a.m. to produce, right after he'd called the human resources manager.

After a few minutes of silence she put the file back on the coffee table and stared at him. 'This is the same contract you signed with Freya.'

'With a few modifications.' Namely the section on children being in the future at a time of his wife's choosing. That was an issue now taken out of both their hands. 'Everything about how our marriage is to proceed is laid out in black and white. There will be no ambiguity and no need for us to argue about any issues at any point in the future because they are all set out in this. You will see that you are also generously provided for.' He would treat her fairly and well. She would be his wife and the mother of his child and he would respect her for both those roles.

Something undefinable sparked in her eyes. 'Your provisions are generous but the rest of it… I'm not signing this.'

He fixed her with the stare that had been known to make an entire conference room of business people freeze. 'If you want me to marry you, you will.'

She shook her head slowly. 'No.'

No. A simple one-syllable word rarely uttered in his earshot and even more rarely directly at him.

He leaned forward and rested his elbows on his thighs. 'Then let me explain it like this. If you won't sign the contract I will not marry you and I will take custody of our child. If you want to be a mother to it then you will sign. Otherwise you can leave right now and stop wasting my time.'

CHAPTER THREE

Sophie stared into the light brown eyes fixed on hers with such hooded cruelty and experienced an unexpected wave of compassion for him.

She didn't want to feel anything for Javier, but right then, how could she not, even when she knew it was her compassion towards him that had got them to this point?

This was a man who had lived through the worst thing a child could live through: the murder of his mother at the hands of his father. Judged and feared by the world, was it any wonder he hit back at it by encasing his heart in steel? She had felt his pain from the first moment she had set eyes on him and fallen under his spell.

He folded his arms across his chest, his stare menacing. 'Well?'

Her heart thundering painfully beneath her ribs, Sophie got to her feet.

Not giving herself time to reflect on what she was doing, she walked around the coffee table and stood before him. Javier was such a tall man and she so short that they were the same height with him seated.

She put her hand to his and locked her fingers around his wrist, feeling him jolt with surprise at her forwardness. His surprise was to her advantage, enabling her to pull his arm free from across his chest and place his hand on her belly.

She tried not to shiver as the heat of his hand permeated through the fabric of her sweater and sent shocks of sensation travelling through her bloodstream.

She had to ignore it.

She should wish she had ignored it two months ago but that would mean wishing her unborn child away and she would never do that.

He tried to pull his hand away but she refused to let go, holding it tightly to her abdomen, grateful for the first time for the physical strength all the ballet training she had endured through her life had given her.

'I know you can't feel it yet but, under your hand, our child is growing inside me,' she said quietly. 'It is over an inch long and has eyes and ears and a mouth. Its fingernails are beginning to grow and it can already bend its arms and legs. You can't feel it but *I* can. My body's changing because of this little kumquat, and our little kumquat is wholly dependent on me. As it grows, it will learn the sound of my voice. If you are by my side it will learn your voice too and when it's born it will recognise both of us. It is innocent of everything and needs us both, so I beg you, please, do not use our child as a weapon to threaten me with. I won't sign that contract because I disagree profoundly with the reasons behind it and I disagree with every one of the clauses you have in it. If we are going to marry then it should be a real marriage.'

Not the cold business arrangement he had made with Freya. That was a marriage Sophie could never tolerate for either herself or her child.

Javier wrenched his hand from her hold, his movement so sudden that Sophie stepped back in shock, straight into the coffee table. She would have toppled backwards onto it if his reflexes hadn't kicked in and the hand he had just snatched from her hadn't flown forward to grip onto her elbow and pull her to him.

She gazed into the eyes holding her with such loathing, greatly aware of the heavy thuds of her heart and the melting of her insides as his tangy scent crept into her senses.

His chest rose and fell at speed, his tanned throat moving, his lips pulling together, nostrils flaring.

For the wildest moment Sophie felt a compulsion to take the one step forward needed to become flush with him.

How could she still react to him like this? He had made love to her, then escorted her out of his home moments later as if she were the carrier of a disease. He had made no effort to contact her when he knew there was a danger he had impregnated her. He'd cared so little that he hadn't noticed that she wasn't on the stage at the theatre opening, had not cared to discover she had left his ballet company.

She should not react like this to him but she would not lie that a part of her wasn't glad she still felt this desire for him. If she was going to get her way and forge a proper marriage with him then they needed a glue to keep them together other than their child.

Javier did not scare her. He probably should. He was a ruthless, coldly arrogant, wildly rich control freak. He'd threatened her with the removal of their child.

But he *was* human. She had experienced his human side, glimpsed the pain in his eyes and knew in her heart that his own heart wasn't so far gone in the dark that his humanity could not be reached.

She would never love him, not now she knew the depths of his cruelty, but, whether they married or not, their unborn child meant they would always be in the other's life.

Javier stared into pale blue eyes with a thousand emotions churning through him. Where had this woman with her calm, compassionate logic that could neuter his arguments come from?

And why the hell was his body straining towards her...?

Disgusted with himself, he released his hold on her elbow, got to his feet and strode away from her.

'I do not want a real marriage,' he told her as he paced. 'What you are asking for is impossible. I like my solitude.'

'We both need to make sacrifices. Speaking on a personal level, you are the last man I would wish to commit my life to but this is not about you or me, this is about our child, who deserves the best life can give. It deserves to be raised with a mother and father who are united. If you're worried that I'm after your money then I am happy to sign an agreement that protects your wealth if we divorce.'

He pounced on her words. 'You are already thinking that far ahead!'

He'd known she couldn't be as self-sacrificing as she was making herself out to be, her words all a script designed to make him feel like a bastard for wanting to protect her from the dangers he posed.

Dios, how could she be so naïve? There was a reason he had reached the age of thirty-five without a single long-term relationship to his name. For a woman proving herself to be far more intuitive than he had credited, she should surely be able to see it.

'If we both enter marriage with open minds we can make it work for our child, I truly believe that,' she replied, following him with her eyes. 'But I am not stupid. The odds are against us and we should work together to protect our child against every eventuality. I will be glad to sign a contract that states that should we divorce the only thing I get from you is a home of my own here in Madrid so we can share custody of our child. I don't want a war with you, Javier, and I absolutely do not want our child to be a casualty of it either. I would have thought you of all people could appreciate that.'

For a moment he stopped pacing to stare at her, stunned.

No one—*no one*—ever alluded to his parents, not to his face.

His parents' marriage had been fodder for the press long before his mother's death. His father, Yuri Abramova, had been a ballet dancer from Moscow from the days of the USSR and had defected to New York in the seventies. Clara had been a Spanish prima ballerina, much younger than her famous husband, whose own fame had soared with her talent until she had eclipsed him in all ways. Their marriage had been volatile and filled with infidelities and jealousy on both sides. Lovers had popped up like cockroaches to sell their stories to an eager press who had known stories of the most famous marriage in the ballet world always sold out its print run.

In the midst of all this toxicity had been two boys who had both suffered but who had got through it by sticking together and protecting the other.

If someone had told the young Javier that his twin, his only confidant, would one day betray him for a woman he would have laughed in their face.

But now their brotherhood was dead, as dead as the mother Javier had worshipped but who had always preferred Luis and as dead as the father who had worshipped Javier and hated Luis.

His entire past was gone. The grandparents who had raised him and Luis after their mother's death and father's incarceration had died within a year of each other a decade ago. Louise Guillem, his mother's closest friend, who had been like an aunt to them, had died seven years ago. Benjamin, Louise's son and Javier and Luis's oldest playmate, was alive and kicking but effectively dead to him.

They were all gone and yet…

Inside this woman who stared unblinkingly back at him, life grew. A child. His child.

An unexpected stab of guilt plunged into his guts.

Sophie was right. Their child was innocent, just as he and Luis had been innocent. His child deserved more than to be used as a weapon before it had grown bigger than his thumb.

Staring hard at the mother of his child, he could see in her eyes that already she loved it enough to fight for its best interests in any way she could. As a child he would have given anything to have been on the receiving end of that kind of love from his own mother.

Was that how Sophie had found the nerve to allude to his childhood and not flinch? How else could she look at him and not recoil in fear at the man who stood before her?

But she hadn't been scared when she had turned up at his door with the same documents he'd had remade early that morning in her name…

Coldly perfect Freya had never displayed any overt fear for him either, but that had been understandable because coldly perfect Freya had never shown any emotions other than on the stage when she came alive in her dance.

Why wasn't Sophie scared of him?

He dragged his fingers down his face and contemplated her some more before nodding slowly. '*Bueno*. I do not know what your expectations of a real marriage are…'

'One that doesn't give the husband a licence to take a mistress for a start,' she interjected drily.

He gaped at this unexpected glimpse of humour. 'You expect fidelity?'

He'd had the clause put in that he could take a mistress if he chose as a black-and-white warning that he was committing to a marriage only on paper. Freya hadn't blinked an eye at it.

'My only expectation is that we both try to make things work.' She expelled a long breath of air and sat back on the sofa. Taking hold of her glass, she gave him a rueful smile. 'All we can do is our best. To be faithful, to be honest, to just…try.'

How could he argue with that? he thought, anger mixing with incredulity.

Sophie had flipped everything on its head and made it all sound so easy.

Did she not see that she was asking the impossible? Javier had no idea if he was capable of fidelity; he'd never had a relationship run long enough for him to find out.

But honesty he could do. He was always honest.

'Do not expect the impossible,' he warned her darkly. 'You know the kind of marriage I had envisaged for myself. I like solitude. I always have and always will. I suspect your idea of a real marriage differs greatly from mine.'

She shrugged. 'The contract makes clear the kind of marriage you want, my refusal to sign it makes clear it's not the marriage I want. We'll both have to make compromises. I'm willing to try if you are.'

For the first time in his adult life Javier found himself in the uncomfortable position of having to bend to someone else's will. With Luis there had been much compromise in the way they ran their business but they had been so in tune with each other's thoughts it had never been an issue. Besides, Luis was his twin. It was a different scenario.

Sophie was only…

The mother of his unborn child.

Damn her, being so reasonable, leaving him little room to manoeuvre.

The thought of sharing his daily life with another person made his skin crawl. The thought of sharing it with this woman made his chest tighten and his stomach cramp.

He made sure her attention was fixed on him before giving a sharp nod. '*Bueno.* We will try it your way, but I warn you now, keep your expectations realistic. I live my life to please myself. This is my home and it is run to suit me. I will make accommodations for our child when it is born, but if you want to enter a marriage where the small details of our lives are not already agreed on then you must live with the consequences when you find the reality not to your liking.'

For the third time in as many months, Sophie approached Javier's front door. This would be her last approach as a visitor. When she stepped through it this time, she would be staying.

This beautiful villa was going to be her home.

This was the best course of action, she told herself firmly, for what had to be the hundredth time.

The past fortnight had passed in a whirl of activity, Sophie busy packing and making arrangements for her new life. She had lived and worked in Madrid for eighteen months but it had never been permanent and she'd lived a minimal life there, always intending to return to England for good when her ballet career was over. Now, embracing that the rest of her life would be spent in Madrid whatever happened in her marriage, she was moving her entire life over.

She had no idea what Javier had been doing since their short meeting where they had thrashed out an agreement that suited neither of them but was best for their child.

She would give their marriage her best shot and she would force him to give it his best too. He had agreed to try. She had to hold onto that even if his actions since she'd returned to England had been less than positive.

He'd politely declined her offer to go to the hospital with her for the first scan, claiming he was too busy, so she had gone with her mother.

Her mother, bless her gentle heart, had been enthralled with the image on the screen. Her father had spent an age staring at the grainy picture she had given him of it. It had broken Sophie's heart to tell the loving couple who had adopted her at eighteen months that their grandchild would be raised in Spain, but she had been able to offset their disappointment by promising lots of visits. She knew it had comforted them to know she would be marrying, although it had been another disappointment to them that they wouldn't meet the groom before the wedding day.

Her poor parents. They'd masked their disappointment at her unplanned pregnancy well but she'd seen the pained glances they'd exchanged before embracing her and offering their full support.

Her parents had both been virgins on their wedding day. Sophie had never expected to stay a virgin until her own but she had been waiting for the thunderbolt they had both told her about, that certainty that she had found 'the one', the man she would spend the rest of her life with. She would never willingly disappoint them with anything less.

Javier was the only man she had looked at and felt her heart and pulses soar.

She had emailed the scan to him but received no response, either positive or negative. His next message to her had been to confirm the date of their wedding, written in the style of a business memo.

The man who had threatened to take full custody of their child if Sophie didn't comply with his demands had so far shown zero interest in it.

She would force an interest. By the time their child was born in six months, she was determined Javier would be as excited for its arrival as she was. She didn't expect miracles. She doubted he would be a hands-on father— the thought of that towering inferno of a man changing a nappy evoked hysterical laughter in her—but for their child's sake she wanted Javier to reach a place where he could open his heart and love it.

She had to believe he was capable of love. She had to.

To be fair to him, he hadn't abandoned her completely. She'd arrived back in the UK to find a chauffeured car waiting for her at the airport, the driver informing her she had him at her disposal until her return to Madrid. When they had settled on the date for her to move in with him, Javier had insisted on sending his private jet to England to collect her. He'd also arranged for a company to collect and transport all her belongings. They should have beaten her here, her stuff all ready for her to unpack in the house she very much hoped would soon feel like home.

Her heart thudded painfully as she took the heavy knocker in her hand, not yet ready to simply walk into this mansion as if she belonged there. She had barely moved it when the door opened.

A thin man in a sober suit greeted her with a nod. 'Miss Johnson, please, come in,' he said in impeccable English. 'I am Julio, Mr Casillas's butler. I run the household staff.'

Sophie tried to stop her eyes popping out of her head.

Javier had a butler? Wow.

On her previous two visits she had seen only one member of staff and had thought little of it. But now she did think about it and realised there was no way a house of these proportions and of such magnificence could be maintained by only one person.

'How many staff are there?' she asked curiously.

'Nine. Three of us live in. Can I get you any refreshment?'

'I ate on the flight over, thank you.'

He smiled. 'Then shall I show you to your room so you can get comfortable?'

'Is Javier not here?'

'Mr Casillas is in a meeting. He will be back this evening.'

She forced a smile to hide the pierce of disappointment. Javier hadn't said he would be at home to meet her. She had made an assumption that he would want to greet her and make her feel welcome because that was what decent men did for the women carrying their child.

She had a feeling this was a deliberate act on Javier's behalf, a throwing down of the gauntlet, a reminder that this marriage was not how he wanted it and he would not have his space encroached.

'Then show me to my room,' she said with artificial brightness. 'Has my stuff arrived yet?'

'It was delivered last night,' he confirmed, leading the way up the grand staircase that spread like wings at the top for the two long sections of the house. He turned right and strode down the wide landing lined with *chaises longues* and cabinets filled with ancient artefacts until he reached the furthest door at the end and opened it for her.

Sophie stepped inside and immediately sucked a breath in.

The room was beautiful.

'I hope you don't mind but we took the liberty of unpacking for you,' Julio said. 'If you are not happy with where your possessions have been put then we will put them where you think more suitable.'

She grinned, her sense of humour tickled at the butler's gravity. 'I'm sure wherever they've been put will be fine and if it's not then I can move them myself.'

'As you wish but please remember we are here to serve. Whatever you require, it is our job to provide it.'

Slowly she gazed around the fabulous room with its three high, wide windows overlooking Javier's beautiful garden, the furthest revealing a glimpse of a swimming pool. She opened a door to find a bathroom bigger than her childhood bedroom, another that revealed a dressing room as large as the living room of the flat she had shared with Freya.

Everything was so soft and clean and feminine…

Narrowing her eyes, she stared harder and walked back into the bathroom.

There was not a single masculine product to be found.

As casually as she could manage, she turned her attention back to the butler, who now stood formally by the bedroom door. 'Where's Javier's room?'

'At the end of the west wing. Would you like me to show you around the rest of the house?'

It placed a great strain on all her facial muscles to pull a smile to her face but she managed it. 'No, thank you, Julio. I'm sure you have work you need to be getting on with. I'm happy to explore on my own.'

'If you are sure?'

'I'm sure.'

After asking once again if she required anything and giving instructions on how to contact the staff for when she did, he left the room, closing the door quietly behind him.

When she was alone, the smile on Sophie's face dropped and she folded her arms protectively around her belly.

So much for them creating a real marriage. Javier had stuck her as far away from him as he could get her.

CHAPTER FOUR

JAVIER SENSED SOPHIE'S presence the moment he stepped through the front door.

There was nothing of her in his eyeline, everything in the same spotless order it was always in, but he could feel her there nonetheless, as if she had arrived and imprinted herself on the walls. If he closed his eyes he could smell her perfume.

All day there had been a tight feeling of impending doom playing in his guts that had distracted his thoughts from the important meeting he'd been holding with his lawyer.

Separating his business interests from Luis's was proving to be much harder than he'd anticipated, almost as hard as wrapping his head around the fact he would be sharing his home with the Englishwoman who carried his child.

In the two weeks since he'd seen her he'd carried on as normal. Apart from booking their wedding, that was.

He'd lodged all the necessary paperwork and arranged for the officiant to marry them here in his home. The ceremony itself would be short and without any fanfare.

In six days' time he would be a married man.

Losing his single status meant nothing to him. He'd always known he would marry when he found the right woman to breed with and continue the Casillas line. Freya had been that right woman, not Sophie. Freya, who would have recoiled at a 'proper' marriage as much as he did.

Not the seemingly sweet, compassionate blonde woman who appeared to have a spine made of much sturdier stuff than he had initially credited her with.

He had never thought about Freya in his private time. Yet Sophie...

She was all he could think about, and as hard as he tried to push her from his thoughts, the harder she pushed back, those wide pale blue eyes staring straight into his whenever he closed his eyes.

She had refused to sign a contract that would have given her an abundance of money each month.

How could anyone be that selfless? It was not possible. Surely it had to be an act?

If it wasn't, if Sophie really was as sweet and giving as she portrayed herself to be, then she would be fragile with it. Sweet things broke easily.

He did not want to break her but she had to understand that he could. The contract he'd wanted her to sign would have protected her as much as him. A person knew where they were with a contract. You signed it and abided by it, something Benjamin had failed to understand when he'd accused Javier and Luis of defrauding him. Benjamin had signed that contract. Javier could not be held responsible for his failure to read it.

Without a detailed contract to knit their marriage together, they would have to forge their own path. Sophie spoke of compromise but that was a meaningless word in itself if both parties looked at compromise with different markers.

He would not allow her to get close to him. Whether she liked it or not, their marriage would never be real in the sense she wanted it to mean.

He looked at his watch and decided to take a shower before dinner and give himself a few minutes of solitude before he had to face her. He would be undisturbed, his staff knowing not to seek him out. Julio ran his household with military precision. Everyone knew their job and did it well.

Treading heavily up the stairs, he loosened his tie from round his neck. He opened his bedroom door, went to step inside and came to an abrupt halt.

Sophie was sitting on the ottoman at the end of his bed, her hand frozen on a stocking she was halfway through rolling up her bare leg.

After a moment's pause she turned to him and smiled. Only the stain of colour on her cheeks betrayed any nerves or fear she might have. 'Good evening, Javier. Have you had a nice day?'

A swell of rage punched through him, which he did not bother to disguise. Propping himself against the doorway, he growled, 'What are you doing in here?'

A small crease formed in her brow. 'It's moving-in day. You sent your private jet to collect me, remember?'

'What are you doing in my bedroom?' he clarified through gritted teeth.

The crease deepened. 'Getting ready for dinner. As it's our first night I thought I would make an effort.' Then she smiled brightly. 'I'm afraid there was a mistake and my stuff had been put in a room on the east wing. I could see how busy your staff were, so I moved it over myself. It didn't take long. I found some empty space in your dressing room to put my clothes in; don't worry, I didn't touch any of your stuff. I'll find space for my books and other bits and pieces tomorrow.'

He had to inhale three times before he could be certain of speaking without hurling obscenities. 'There was no mistake.'

'Yes, there was.'

'No mistake. My staff put you in the room I designated for your use.'

'Oh, I do apologise for the confusion. I didn't mean your staff had made a mistake in where they put me. I meant *you* had made a mistake.' Then, dropping her eyes from his gaze, she rolled the stocking up over her knee and to her thigh, then patted the lacy top of it to keep it in place. 'I've never worn hold-ups before,' she added conversationally. 'I normally wear tights but they've started getting a little tight around my belly and I'm not ready for maternity wear yet. I hope they don't fall down.'

Her nonchalance, her *nerve*, were astounding.

Javier gritted his teeth even tighter and cursed himself for allowing his eyes to take in the milky-white thigh now encased in black lace.

Sexy lingerie had never done anything for him and he could not believe his blood was pumping harder to see it on her.

But, *Dios*, she was sitting on his antique ottoman, her cherubic looks and hair reminiscent of an angel, her blood-red dress, modestly cut though it was, reminiscent of a vampire. His grinding teeth were taken with the compulsion to sink into the milky flesh still exposed over the top of the lacy hold-ups…

He clenched his hands into fists.

This stopped right now. Whatever game Sophie was playing ended here. She had tempted him once, dressed only as a waif, had driven him to a place he had never gone before and which he had regretted the moment it was over.

Healthy desire was good. Sex was good. Choosing the right person to have sex with was what made it good, a person you desired on a physical level, who made your loins tighten but with whom your heart kept its normal beat. A woman you could walk away from and never have to think about or consider again. A woman with whom wearing a condom was at the forefront of your mind, not a cursed afterthought when it was all over.

'This is my bedroom,' he said tightly. 'My private space. You have been given your own bedroom for your own private space.'

'Your house is big enough for us to both host individual parties without disturbing the other, so I would say there's plenty of space to escape to if we get on each other's nerves.'

'Do not be flippant,' he snarled.

Sophie got to her feet and smoothed the red dress she had donned because it was her only decent dress that still fitted properly with her growing breasts, praying he didn't notice the tremors in her hands and that he couldn't see the beats of her frantically beating heart.

Why did he have to walk in when she'd been putting the hold-ups on? Julio had told her Javier was expected home at seven p.m. but he had arrived back half an hour early. She'd wanted to be ready for him, be sitting on the light grey sofa that backed along the far wall, fully dressed.

She still didn't know how she'd found the nerve to move her stuff over to his bedroom. She had sat alone for almost an hour mulling over her options on how best to proceed. Should she stay in her designated room at the furthest point from his and hope that at some point in the future she would be allowed to join him in it? Or should she fight from the start for the marriage she wanted and which he had promised to try for?

The latter had won and now she had to brazen it out.

Standing as tall as her five-foot-nothing frame would allow, she stared up at his towering six-foot-plus form. 'I know you and Freya were only going to share a bed one night a week but that is not something I can contemplate. That is not a marriage.'

She remembered feeling sick to read that contract when

it had been designed with Freya in mind, the flash of jealousy that had wracked Sophie to imagine her best friend in the arms of the man she had developed such strong feelings for. To see it replicated in her own contract had filled her with despair.

'I am aware you work long hours and travel a lot for your business, so the evenings are often going to be the only times we share together,' she continued. 'How can we form any kind of bond if we're in separate wings of your house?'

'If it's sex you require then I can accommodate that without you moving into my personal space.' His eyes flashed dangerously as he finally crossed the threshold of the huge, luxurious bedroom and kicked the door shut behind him. Walking towards her in slow, long strides, like a big cat stalking towards its prey, he put his hands to the buckle of his belt. 'If it is relief you are after then take your dress off and I will satisfy it for you.'

'Sex is a part of it,' she answered, refusing to be intimidated by this power play instinct told her was designed to frighten her, 'but I'm talking about intimacy.'

He stopped a foot away from her, his face contorted. 'I do not *do* intimacy.'

'But that's what a real marriage entails. If you won't share a bedroom with me then it proves you're not willing to try like you promised you would and, if that is the case, I might as well have our baby in England, where I will get the support I need—'

'You dare threaten me?' he cut through her, his incredulity obvious.

'I would *never* threaten you,' she said, horrified he would think her capable of such a thing.

'You just threatened to return to England with our baby.'

'Only until it's born.' She sat back on the ottoman and threaded her fingers through her hair as she tried to explain her thoughts without getting so emotional that the tears started falling.

Javier was so ice-like that it felt as if she were trying to get through to a sculpture.

'I haven't made this move for my sake but for our child's. If I was thinking only of my own interests I would have stayed in England and had my parents' support throughout the pregnancy. I don't expect miracles, but if you won't share a bed with me when that's the most basic part of a marriage then what's the point? I made it very clear that I want a real marriage and this for me is it. Sharing a bed. Getting to know each other, and getting to a point that when our child is born we're comfortable together and united. That's my red line. I need you to prove your commitment. Either we share a bed or we forget about marriage because it will be far more damaging for our child to be born in an unhappy home than be born to two separate but content homes. Our child can still have your name because I know that's important for you. I'll be happy to live in Madrid after the birth so we can share custody. You can still be a father even if you won't be a husband.'

Javier listened to Sophie speak knowing she'd outmanoeuvred him again with her damned reasonableness.

She was giving him a way out of their marriage and if he had any sense he would take it.

'Do you know what my experience of a real marriage is?' he asked harshly, sitting on the edge of the bed so she was only a blur in the corner of his eye. 'My parents.'

He heard her suck an intake of breath. 'I know that to call your childhood hard would be an understatement but I don't want our baby to suffer for it. I'm not asking you to commit emotionally to me, Javier. I am asking you to commit emotionally to our child.'

He thought of the scan she'd emailed to him the week before. He'd stared at it for so long his eyes had blurred.

Their baby. Their innocent baby, who had no idea what kind of a father it had been burdened with.

He'd been prepared to leave the raising of any child he had with Freya in her hands. Sophie, he suspected, would want him to be involved.

Sophie, who wanted him to share a bed with her every night. To share a space.

Dios, he hadn't shared personal space since he and Luis had left their grandparents' home when they'd turned eighteen to set out on their own, determined even at that young age to earn themselves a fortune. They had rented a small two-bedroom apartment and for the first time in his life Javier had found himself with a room to call his own. The freedom had been like learning to breathe for the first time.

He thought hard before rolling his neck and taking a sharp breath. '*Bueno*. You win. We will try it your way and share a bedroom but only here in this house. I have made it very clear what my own red lines are. I need my solitude. I am a loner and I will never change. I dislike company. When I travel on business, you will not be invited to accompany me, so don't waste your time thinking of arguments for why you should. I have no need for a confidante, so do not expect me to pour my heart out to you. If I wish to go out for an evening on my own do not expect me to take you with me. If I tell you I need space then I expect you to respect that.'

'I will respect all of that,' she promised.

'Good.' He nodded tightly and got to his feet. 'Excuse me but I need to shower before dinner.'

He strode to the bathroom before she could object, needing to get away from Sophie and that floral fragrance she wore that had already permeated the walls of his bedroom.

She might have inveigled herself into it but he was damned if he would let her get a foot in any other aspect of his life.

He could manage nights with her, he reasoned. After all, night-time was for sleeping.

He would dine out more frequently, he decided. Work even longer hours than he already did, hit his personal gym with more vigour, exhaust himself so greatly that when he did rest his head beside hers he would not care that Sophie and her sinfully tempting body lay there. He would simply fall asleep.

'Is Luis going to be your best man?' Sophie asked when she could bear the silence no more.

They'd finished their first course of cured meats and accompaniments and were now eating their main course. They'd been sitting in the dining room for half an hour and Javier had hardly exchanged a word with her. Her every attempt at conversation had been met with monosyllabic answers and grunts.

To make the tension in her stomach even worse, this was the very table he had made love to her on.

It felt so long ago now it could have been a different life but being in here with him brought back memories and feelings that had been smothered under the weight of the fear she had carried with her since, from the horrifying realisation they had failed to use protection to the terrifying realisation she was pregnant with his child.

His lips tightened but he didn't look up from his phone, which he was typing on with his left hand while working his fork absently between his food and his mouth with the other. 'No.'

His own twin wasn't going to be his best man? 'Who is, then?'

'I'm not having one.'

'Why not?'

'I have no need for one. We do not need guests. Our wedding ceremony will be quick and serve a function.'

Not need guests? What kind of a wedding would it be without them?

'I've already invited my parents.'

'Un-invite them.'

Sophie put her fork down, folded her arms across her chest and stared at him for so long that eventually he noticed and flickered his eyes at her.

'I am not getting married without my parents,' she told him flatly. 'It wouldn't be fair. They've already booked their flights.'

His jaw clenched. 'Have you told them they can stay here?'

Do I look stupid? she wanted to retort, settling instead on 'They're booked in a hotel.'

He stared at her for so long tumbleweed could have crossed the huge dining room twice. 'Have you invited anyone else without consulting me?'

'I didn't realise I needed permission to invite my parents to our wedding.'

'Consultation is not the same as permission.'

'I quite agree, which is why I think it's outrageous you've decided we should have no guests at all without any consultation with me.'

She did not drop her stare. Respect worked both ways and he needed to learn that.

A pulse throbbed in his temple.

Javier, she realised, was so tightly wound that to pull him any tighter would make him snap.

It didn't scare her. Javier needed to snap. It could not be healthy keeping everything bottled inside him all the time.

'I am very close to my parents,' she told him in a gentler tone when he made no effort to respond. 'It would break their hearts if I married without them.'

His lips pulled together before he finally inclined his head.

'*Bueno*, your parents can come.'

She bit back the words of thanks she wanted to say. Gratitude on this would make her look weaker than he already thought her to be.

The sooner Javier came to regard her as his equal, the better.

She had a feeling that with the exception of his brother, he rarely saw anyone as equal to him. Freya had gained his respect, she thought with a pang that felt suspiciously like jealousy, but then Freya was the female version of Javier; single-minded and driven.

If Sophie could cut through Freya's walls then she could at least chip away at Javier's.

By the time their child was born she would have chipped away at enough of it that he could be the loving father their child needed and deserved.

Taking her cutlery back in her hand, she cut a bite of the delicious pork fillet and added some of the red pepper and chorizo sauce.

Eighteen months in Madrid had given Sophie a great appreciation of its culture but its food had been something she'd limited herself with, her ballet diet too strict for her to dare eat out much. It had been safer to prepare all her own tried and tested meals and ignore the tantalising aromas that had greeted her whenever she'd stepped onto Madrid's bustling streets. She had missed out on so much but what surprised her was how little she had missed dancing since she'd quit.

She'd been so ashamed of what she'd done with Javier that she had left the company the next day. By the time she'd taken the pregnancy test she'd known she would never dance professionally again. Without the drive of constant performances and tours to keep her in top condition and with the tiredness that had drained her in the early weeks of pregnancy, her exercise regime had gone from seven intense hours a day minimum to hardly anything.

And she didn't miss it at all. She found it liberating in a way she'd never anticipated. She could eat the wonderful salt-baked new potatoes that made her taste buds tingle in delight without an ounce of guilt.

The magical food Javier's chef had created deserved to be appreciated much more than Javier currently was appreciating it, his attention again back on his phone.

'Is Luis coming to the wedding?' she asked before popping the fork into her mouth.

Start as she meant to go on, she reminded herself. This was *their* wedding. She'd been happy to leave the arrangements in Javier's hands but she would not exchange her vows blind to everything.

He didn't look up. 'No.'

'Is he too busy?'

His shoulders rose and his nostrils flared before he answered. 'Luis and I are finished, as brothers and business partners, and if you would stop asking me inane questions I could respond to this email my lawyer has sent me about it.'

The Casillas brothers were finished? Had she really heard that correctly?

The tightness of his features proved she had not misheard.

'What's happened?' she asked quietly. She would not allow his bad temper to push her into silence. Sophie had dealt with temperamental dancers and choreographers her entire life and had long ago stopped being silenced by anger.

Anger always went hand in hand with pain, something she had learned at the age of nine when her paternal grandmother had died. It was the only time her father had ever lashed out. A normal Sunday dinner in the weeks after the funeral became a memory of a plate full of food smashing into the wall, her father offended by the lack of seasoning, ranting, face red and furious, shouting obscenities Sophie had never heard before. Her mother had watched in silence, then had gone to him and taken him in her arms.

The howl of pain her father had given as he'd collapsed into her mother's arms was a sound Sophie would remember for the rest of her life.

Javier's sharp eyes suddenly found hers again 'Luis's engagement to Chloe Guillem was announced a week ago. Is that explanation enough?'

'Benjamin's *sister*?' Not just Benjamin's sister but a costume maker employed by Compania de Ballet de Casillas.

He nodded and took a drink of his water.

'Didn't you say she'd been involved in Benjamin stealing Freya away from you?' She was sure he had, right before they had made love on this table. He had made her coffee and asked her the questions she'd guessed had been playing on his mind for a week. She'd been sad for him that she couldn't answer them but, in truth, she'd been as surprised as he'd been by what Freya had done.

Freya didn't love Javier but she'd been desperate for the money marrying him would have given her, which she had planned to spend on an expensive experimental treatment for her mother, who had a rare neurological disease. The treatment wouldn't have saved her life but there was a chance it would extend and improve the quality of it.

'Chloe conspired with her brother to make Luis and myself late for the gala, which enabled Benjamin to pounce and steal Freya away to his chateau in France.'

'And Luis is now engaged to her? How does that work?'

His eyes glittered with menace. 'My brother's loyalty has transferred to the Guillems. I'm surprised you haven't read about it. The press have loved reporting that latest twist in the saga.'

'I've been avoiding the news since I went home to England,' she admitted. 'That doorstepping left a very unpleasant taste in my mouth.'

Javier stared at her, suddenly remembering the strange protective feeling that had raced through him when she'd spoken of the press harassment. And with it came the memory of how his eyes had been unable to do anything but drink her in.

He could keep his eyes fixed to his phone as much as he liked but every nerve ending in his body was aware of the woman seated opposite him and every muscle remembered with painful intensity the sensation of being burrowed deep inside her.

'Luis is a traitor,' he answered flatly, speaking aloud the fury coiling like a viper inside him for the first time.

It was not the press Sophie needed protecting from, it was him.

Sophie needed to know who she was marrying.

'I have protected him since childhood and carried him through the business and he repays me by defending and choosing to marry the woman who conspired with her brother to destroy us. He is dead to me and I would thank you not to mention his name in my presence again.'

Her eyes widened, whether at his tone or his words he did not know or care.

When it came to his brother, there would be no compromise.

Luis could rot in hell.

CHAPTER FIVE

SOPHIE LAY IN Javier's huge bed fighting to keep her eyes open. She must have lain there for an hour waiting for him, thrills of different shades racing through her: terror, excitement, nausea, until eventually they all melded into one that tasted of disappointment.

When she had climbed into the bed, she had thought he would soon follow. They'd finished their first meal together with him telling her to go up and make use of the bathroom before he joined her. She'd thought he was being considerate and giving her a little privacy. She didn't need to tell him she'd never brushed her teeth around a man before or taken a shower near one. He would know.

She sighed.

It was only her first day there. She had to remember that. Javier had huge adjustments to make, fundamental ones that, she suspected, went far deeper than her own.

Building a bond would not happen overnight. It would take time. He was not a man who trusted easily and he was having to cope with a heck of a lot; the humiliation of Freya leaving him for Benjamin, Sophie being pregnant with his child, marrying her and now the destruction of his relationship with his twin.

She wished she had known about that. It would have made her think twice about asking about Luis.

She sighed again, the sigh turning into a wide yawn.

Her eyes were getting really heavy. Much longer and she'd be asleep.

Pregnancy had brought about many changes in her: weight gain, the sudden appearance of breasts, the softening of muscles that had always been hard, but the tiredness had been the biggest challenge. Usually she had bagfuls of energy. In the early weeks she'd found herself nodding off so frequently she'd done an Internet search asking if narcolepsy was a pregnancy side effect. The tiredness had got better in recent weeks but she wasn't back to her normal energy levels yet. She'd had a full and busy day, physically and emotionally, and now her body craved nothing but sleep.

Five more minutes.

She would try to stay awake for five more minutes…

Javier stood at his bedroom doorway and breathed deeply.

The air felt different. The only illumination, which came from the dim bedside light on Sophie's side, the side he usually slept, felt softer.

Treading onto the carpet, he felt the thick ply beneath his bare feet in a way he'd never felt it before.

How could the bedroom he'd slept in for five years feel so *different*?

There was no movement from the mound burrowed under his bedsheets.

She'd fallen asleep, just as he'd hoped.

To be sure, he went to her side and peered down. If she was awake he would ask her to move over to the other side.

The sheets swaddled her, her pretty face peeking out, locks of blonde hair spread in different directions over the pillow.

She breathed deeply, the serene sleep of an innocent, oblivious to him staring so intently at her, unaware of his hand hovering closer…

He shoved his hand into his pocket, turned on his heel and, his heart thundering, went into the bathroom, locking the door behind him.

He'd been seconds from stroking her face.

The hour he'd spent pounding his punching bag and running on his treadmill had done nothing to dent his awareness of her.

Her mere presence at the dining table had dragged what should have been a relatively simple email exchange with his lawyer over the entire meal, Sophie snatching his attention even when she wasn't pulling him into conversation.

He'd felt the blood pumping through his veins in a way he had never felt it before, still there, racing through him, alive, with every beat of his heart.

His awareness of the waif-like ballerina was becoming torturous.

Dios, awareness of a beautiful woman was one thing, a healthy thing, but this was something else entirely, as if something with its own heartbeat had infected his blood.

The thought of climbing into bed with Sophie with all this awareness simmering in him had been unthinkable.

He cursed under his breath.

When they made love, he needed to approach it as he always did, from a place of detachment, make it the mechanical exercise sex had always been for him.

'Detached' was not a word to describe how he felt with Sophie under his roof.

Sex with her had not been a mechanical exercise.

It had been mind-blowing. He had carried the feelings it had brought about in him for weeks after, even when he'd refused to allow Sophie herself into his thoughts.

It was only because she'd caught him at such a low point, he reasoned grimly as he brushed his teeth. It had been the perfect storm. An empty house. A beautiful woman with a sympathetic ear and compassionate eyes.

What man wouldn't have reacted in such a manner in that situation and with a woman who had melted at his first touch?

Those feelings had gone eventually, and the feeling of new life in his blood would disappear eventually too.

What else could he do to speed up the detachment? He'd worked out, taken a cold shower in the basement changing room he'd had installed next to his gym, and it had done nothing.

He stripped off his clothes with the exception of his boxers. He always slept nude but tonight that would not be an option, not until he'd got a grip of all these...*feelings*.

He cursed again.

Feelings were dangerous. Especially for him.

Sophie opened her eyes.

Something had woken her.

Then she heard faint sound coming from the bathroom and her heart began to pound.

Javier was in there.

He had finally deigned to join her.

Yawning, she groped for her phone to check the time, blinked and looked again.

She'd been alone in this bed for two hours.

In her heart she knew he'd intentionally waited all this time. He *wanted* her to be asleep.

For the first time it occurred to her that the reason Javier didn't want to share a bed with her was nothing to do with his craving for solitude but because he simply did not fancy her. She'd been nothing but a convenient, willing release for him with huge unintended consequences.

The bathroom door opened. She squeezed her eyes back shut and held her breath.

She sensed rather than heard him tread to the bed.

There was only the slightest of dips as he climbed into

it, then settled himself down with his back to her, keeping a distance that could only be breached deliberately. A moment later the room plunged into darkness.

How long she waited for him to do or say something she could not guess. Time lost its meaning in the dark.

There was no movement from him as the time dragged on. No sound either. Nothing. It was like lying beside an empty vessel.

While she had tried hard to stop herself assuming anything about what the night would bring, she'd been unable to stop herself making the fatal assumption that he would hold her in his arms and, at the very least, touch her stomach holding their growing child within its secure confines.

'Goodnight, Javier,' she whispered in the darkness.

There was no answer.

The following five days passed in a flash. It was a passage Sophie would remember as being a time of blurring nothing.

She spent the days themselves wandering around Javier's villa and gardens, familiarising herself with everything, trying her hardest to feel comfortable within the spacious halls and learn more about the man she was soon to marry. This was her home, she constantly reminded herself. She should not feel like an unwanted trespasser.

The only things she learned about the man himself were that he had a penchant for ancient artefacts and no need for mirrors. In this villa that contained eleven bedrooms and twelve bathrooms, the reflective surfaces were confined to internal glass walls and doors, and shaving mirrors. The only bedroom with a full-length mirror was the one she'd been initially designated.

Things would be easier to manage and cope with if Javier didn't continue to keep her at arm's length. He left for work early and on three of the evenings failed to make it home in time for dinner, leaving her to dine alone. He would make a point of saying hello to her when he arrived back but would then disappear, joining her in the bedroom when, she knew, he hoped she would be asleep.

He made no effort to touch her. Sophie would find herself lying wide awake in the darkness psyching herself to turn over and put a hand to the cold shoulder facing her.

She didn't think he slept either. He was just too still.

If she had more confidence she would say something but every time she opened her mouth her throat would close. She didn't know the words to say without making herself sound like a needy nymphomaniac.

He was doing as she'd asked and sharing a bed with her. If he didn't desire her she couldn't force it.

Or was it something else? It hadn't been just the contract he'd wanted her to sign that stated they would share a bed only one night of the week, but the contract he'd drawn up for Freya too.

Could it be simply that Javier had no interest in sex?

The conception of their child proved the lie in that, not just its conception but the way it had been conceived. Sophie had been a virgin but she had also spent her life in the hotbed of the ballet world, where passions always ran high. She knew passion when she saw it and in Javier's arms she had felt it, had tasted it in his kisses.

Whatever lay behind his reluctance to touch her and however many times she told herself that it was early days and to give it time, Sophie's hopes of creating a bond with him were fading.

The arrival of her parents brought some happiness into her heart and she spent the day before her wedding with them, plastering a smile to her face, keeping up the pretence that everything was fine and that this was a marriage she was entering with high expectations that it would last.

Luckily, Sophie was a pro at convincing her parents

that everything was rosy. Their love and pride had given her the focus to get through ballet school and work like a Trojan to succeed in the ballet world. Her first concrete memory was of her mother clapping her hands in delight to see four-year-old Sophie perform in her first ballet recital. Her pride had filled Sophie's heart and been the kick-start to the rest of her life.

Through dance she could make the woman who had given her a home and showered her with love beam with happiness.

The nights when she would lie awake yearning for the path her heart wanted would be put aside when the morning came. She would fix the image of her parents in her head and drag herself out of bed to start another day.

On that last day as a single woman, she was enjoying a meal out with them when her phone rang.

She would have been less surprised if it had been the Spanish prime minister calling.

The restaurant being too loud to hear, Sophie excused herself and went outside to call Javier back.

'Where are you?' he asked, picking up on the first ring.

'In a tapas bar with my parents,' she answered, surprised to hear what could be interpreted as brusque concern in his voice.

'Where?'

She named the street and district. 'Do you want to join us?'

'No. Why didn't you use my driver?'

'I didn't know I could. I took a taxi. Why do you sound so cross?'

'I'm not cross.' He sounded affronted at the mere thought. 'When will you be back?'

'Tomorrow. I've checked into my parents' hotel. They've brought the wedding dress over, so it makes sense for me to stay with them.'

'I should have been consulted on this.'

'It was only decided today. I was going to call you later to tell you.' She looked at her watch. It was eight thirty.

'*Tell* me?' he said dangerously.

Sophie rolled her eyes at his double standards. 'Considering you do as you please with no consultation with me, you're hardly in a position to moan when I do the same.'

The line went silent until he said tightly, 'So this was punishment for me working hard?'

A wave of weariness washed over her and she took a seat on a nearby bench. 'No, Javier, it wasn't a punishment. You haven't been home earlier than nine o'clock these past three nights. I didn't want to disturb you while you were working. I was trying to be considerate.'

Another lengthy pause. 'Next time, disturb me or message me.'

'Okay. But if you want me to account for my movements, it's only fair if you do the same.'

A grunt played into her ear before he said, 'Message me the details of the hotel. I'll send my driver to collect you in the morning.'

'Not too early,' she interjected. 'My mum says it's bad luck for us to see each other before the ceremony.'

The grunt he gave this time had a tinge of impatience to it. 'He will collect you at eleven. Enjoy your evening.'

'What are...?'

But she never got to ask him what his own plans for the evening were because the line had gone dead.

Sophie put her phone to her chest and closed her eyes, the beginning of a smile forming on her lips.

It had never occurred to her that Javier would come home at a decent time and that he would be worried to find her missing. She'd thought the only thing he would feel was relief to have the place to himself.

Her legs felt much lighter when she walked back into the restaurant. Her chest felt lighter too.

Javier had worried about her, and even if his concern had been because she was the vessel that carried his child, it still meant that, in his own way, he was beginning to care.

Javier splashed the remnants of shaving foam off his face, then turned his back on the small mirror and patted his face dry as he walked into the empty bedroom.

He could not believe how heavy his limbs had become. His chest felt as if a lead weight were compressing it.

He dressed methodically, underwear, white shirt, charcoal trousers, navy silk tie, then sat on the unmade bed to put on the hand-stitched shoes he'd had buffed and polished.

He'd expected to sleep well without Sophie lying beside him and catch up on all the sleep her presence had denied him this past week.

He could curse. With or without her fragrant body beside him, sleep had become a foe.

The one good thing was he'd been able to reclaim his usual side of the bed but that had turned into a bad thing because the sheets hadn't been stripped and so he'd spent the night inhaling her perfume that clung to her pillow. Chucking the pillow on the floor and using his own had done nothing to help because by then her scent had crept into his senses and stuck there. He'd still been able to smell her when he woke after a few snatched hours.

At least he hadn't felt compelled to lie like a statue all night. He could spread his limbs out, roll over, all the usual things a person did in the comfort of their bed without having to worry about accidentally finding a part of himself brushing against Sophie's silky skin.

Dressed, he went back in the bathroom to tame his

hair. Usually he made quick work of it, never meeting his own eye.

Today, he dipped his fingers into the pot of wax and stared hard at the reflection he despised but which his father had delighted in.

His father would stand beside him at a mirror and smile with satisfaction at the similarities.

'You are my son,' he would purr in the Slavic accent Javier had come to detest.

If Javier had more closely resembled his mother as Luis had done, would his father still have purred? Or would he have despised him as he had despised Luis?

His father's love of him had been superficial at best, a form of narcissism, its value worthless. It hadn't stopped his father beating Luis, even in the younger years when Javier would cry and beg him to stop. His tears had only made his father hit harder.

He had trained himself not to cry, to hold the emotion in and concentrate his energy on keeping his troublemaking twin out of the escapades that always evoked their father's wrath, his punishments delivered with a gleam that had made Javier sure he enjoyed dispensing them.

And his, Javier's face was the face his father had delighted in looking at, Javier the son he'd felt the affinity with, the child he'd believed was *just like him*.

How could Sophie look at that face and not recoil? Was she so blind she couldn't see the danger in it?

There was a knock on his bedroom door.

'Come in,' he called out brusquely.

Julio appeared. 'The officiant has entered the grounds.'

Javier nodded and worked the wax into his hair. 'And Michael?' he asked, referring to his driver.

'At Sophie… Miss Johnson's hotel.'

He gave his reflection one last look.

It was time to get married.

* * *

Sophie thanked whoever or whatever had looked out for her since her birth for her parents. Their excitement on this, her wedding day, was infectious and did much to curb the nerves chewing in her belly.

As Javier's driver pulled up outside the villa, her mother practically squealed with excitement. 'This is your *home*?'

Unable to speak, Sophie nodded.

The excited chatter between her parents fell to awed silence when they entered the house. Julio and one of the maids greeted them with smiles that didn't quite meet their eyes. If anything, their smiles could be interpreted as sympathetic, which sent alarm bells ringing in her.

Her father holding her arm tightly, they followed Julio through the house, aglow with autumn sunshine pouring through the beautiful intricate skylights, until they reached the orangery.

The orangery was one of Sophie's favourite rooms and she'd been delighted when Javier had suggested they marry in it. More a giant conservatory than anything else, when its doors and windows were open the most wonderful scents from the garden filled it.

She'd not allowed her expectations of what the orangery would be transformed into for this day run away with her but neither had she allowed herself to think about stepping into it and wanting to burst into tears.

The only difference in the orangery was that an oak desk had been placed in the centre with a handful of chairs facing it, presumably for her parents and their witnesses, Julio and his partner, to sit on.

There were no flowers, no balloons, nothing to indicate what an important event this was.

She took it all in slowly with a heart that wanted to smash out of her chest.

If she'd realised that there was to be no effort whatsoever she would never have worn this dress. She would have worn a pair of jeans and trainers.

A quick and functional ceremony was one thing but this…

This was humiliating.

She felt like an imposter, she realised with a wrench. The wrong bride.

Freya, whom in a fit of guilt Sophie had messaged that morning confessing her pregnancy and warning of their marriage, knowing when the press discovered it they would start hounding her and Benjamin all again, was supposed to have stood there.

The man who waited for her, his back currently turned to her—no change there—as he spoke to the rotund officiant, would never have made the choice to marry Sophie if it weren't for the baby.

She wouldn't want to marry him if it were not for the baby either, she reminded herself. Her body still yearned for him but her pounding heart would never yearn for him again. Her heart had learned its lesson, and thank God it had because this would have broken it.

The only effort he'd made was to don a suit. An ordinary suit. The kind of suit he wore every day for work.

And then he turned around and his eyes met hers.

The pounding of her heart became a thrum that vibrated through to her bones.

Javier's mouth had run dry.

He stared at Sophie, hardly able to believe what his eyes were showing him.

He'd never imagined she would wear a traditional wedding dress.

He'd never imagined she could look so beautiful or that his heart would thump so hard the beats could be heard by anyone who listened.

White lace skimmed across her collarbones, forming long fitted sleeves to her wrists, the long lace-wrapped silk dress itself hugging her figure like a caress.

She didn't look pregnant. She looked like a curvaceous nymph and as ravishing a sight as he had ever seen.

He inhaled deeply as he tried to get his thoughts in order.

But she had blown him away.

Pale blue eyes shone back at him.

Suddenly he realised why they were shining. They brimmed full of unshed tears.

That knowledge brought him back to his senses.

He inhaled deeply again, this time fighting anger.

Sophie had no reason to be upset. He'd explicitly told her the ceremony would be quick and functional. She'd chosen not to listen.

But then he watched her demeanour change. Her shoulders lifted and her neck elongated as she raised her chin and said, 'Are we going to do this?'

He stared at her for a further brief moment before nodding.

Yes. It was time to marry this blindingly beautiful woman and give the full protection of his name and wealth to the growing life inside her.

They stood side by side in front of the officiant and, as the quick and functional ceremony began, the weight that had been compressing in his chest since he'd awoken sank lower into him.

For the first time since he'd cut Luis from his life he felt his absence.

He'd never thought he would marry without his brother beside him.

And he'd never thought he would marry with a maelstrom of feelings erupting in him strong enough to knock him off his feet.

He almost choked his vows out.

By contrast, Sophie's Spanish was flawless and her sultry voice carried clearly. He pressed his palms against his thighs to prevent them reaching for her until it was time to exchange rings.

She held her hand out to him.

He took a deep breath and took it into his own.

Her hand was delicate. The nails on the elegant fingers were smooth and polished, the skin soft and dewy.

This time he was not quick enough to shake the stab of guilt away before it could plunge into him.

Sophie had made a huge effort for this occasion. Her actions had shown him more clearly than any words could that this was a commitment she took seriously.

He slid the ring onto her finger knowing she deserved so much more than the man she was pledging herself to.

Then it was her turn to put the ring on his finger.

His father had never worn a wedding ring. For that reason alone, Javier would wear one.

She took his hand gently in hers and then, her eyes gazing right into his, pushed the cold metal over his knuckle.

Its weight hit him like a physical mark to his person.

He stared down at it.

Where for thirty-five years there had been nothing, a gold band now lay.

Her fingers tightened around his.

Suddenly he became aware of expectant eyes upon him. The officiant's, Sophie's parents'…

And Sophie herself. Except hers weren't expectant, they were pleading.

He could read everything contained in those pale blue eyes that shone beautifully under the bright sun filtering through the glass roof.

For my parents' sake, please kiss me, her eyes beseeched.

Kiss her?

She should be pleading with him to never touch her again.

The weight pressing down inside him increased, making it hard for him to draw breath.

He had to kiss her.

A kiss to seal their marriage and spare her humiliation was the least she deserved from him.

Tightening his fingers around hers as hers were clasped around his, he placed his other hand lightly against her waist and lowered his face to hers.

There was not a sound to be heard. Only the thrashing of his heart.

Holding his breath, he pressed his lips to her mouth.

The thrashing turned into a heavy thud.

The floor he stood upon began to sink beneath him and he had to dig deeply all the way from his toes to keep himself grounded and not sink with it, not give in to the nerve endings all straining to her.

He counted to five, then pulled away.

Then he made the mistake of looking at her.

That beautiful face, cheeks slashed with colour, eyes wide...

He forced air into his lungs.

Her perfume fell in with it.

He shuddered and, gritting his teeth, turned back to the officiant.

He had done his duty. Now it was time to sign the document that would confirm them legally as husband and wife.

CHAPTER SIX

SOPHIE EMBRACED HER father tightly, holding onto the wonderful feeling of safety that engulfed her for the last time.

This was a different goodbye from all the others they'd shared. Before, there had always been the knowledge that Sophie would return, not necessarily to her parents' home but to England, somewhere close enough that their lives would entwine again.

Living in Madrid as she intended to do for at least the next eighteen years, that would not be possible.

Then she embraced her mother and squeezed her even harder.

Without these dear, loving people taking her into their hearts and their home, who knew how her life would have turned out? She owed them everything.

And then they were gone, bursting with happiness for their only child, their blinkers well and truly switched on, seeing exactly what they wanted to see, as they had always done and as Sophie had always enabled.

They had watched her perform hundreds of times, blissfully unaware that her heart had yearned to be elsewhere.

Now they had seen her marry a fabulously wealthy man, seen the home she would raise their grandchild in, and that had been enough for them to leave with contented hearts.

If either thought it strange that neither had had the nerve to embrace their new son-in-law, their faces hadn't shown it.

Sophie turned her head.

Javier was leaning against his giant sphinx artefact, his arms loosely crossed over his stomach. He'd removed his jacket and tie during the horrendously awkward meal they'd shared with her parents. The meal hadn't been pre-planned. He'd snapped his fingers and ordered it to be done after they'd exchanged their vows and before Sophie had had the humiliation of telling her parents the celebrations they expected were not happening. A bottle of champagne had been produced, the first alcoholic drink served since Sophie had moved in. Javier had stuck to the same sparkling grape juice that she'd consumed.

Sophie thought hard, trying to remember if he'd drunk alcohol in front of her at all, but came up blank. Was he being considerate of her pregnant state?

Somehow she could not believe that to be the reason. Javier would not make a concession like that when he barely knew what the word 'concession' meant and refused point-blank to learn it.

But he had arranged the meal and raised a toast to his bride, all for her parents' benefit.

Maybe he did have a conscience in that steel heart of his.

She sighed. 'I'm going to have a bath and go to bed.'

He nodded but made no verbal answer.

She wished she could read him but he was impossible to interpret. She had never known anyone so capable of keeping their thoughts and emotions hidden.

Did he even have emotions? That was something she was beginning to doubt.

But she thought she'd seen something in his eyes when he'd given her that fleeting kiss right after they'd exchanged their wedding rings.

He hadn't touched her since, not even an accidental brush of his arm to hers.

She ran the bath and added a good dollop of scented bubble bath to it, watching the foam develop in the swirling water, determined not to cry.

When it had filled sufficiently, she walked back through the bedroom to the dressing room and armed herself with a pair of pyjamas, her oldest, most comfortable pair. Javier wouldn't care that they were as sexy as a clown's outfit. She'd worn her prettiest nightdresses all week and he hadn't even cared to look at her in them.

She was about to step back into the bathroom when a vibrating sound caught her attention and a quick look found her phone on the bedroom table. A member of the staff must have put it there. She'd forgotten all about it, not having used it since at the hotel with her parents that morning.

She turned it on to find three returned messages from Freya.

She read the first.

What? Sophie, you CANNOT marry Javier. He will eat you alive. Come to France. We'll take care of you and the baby.

The second:

Call me.

Then the third—the one she'd heard vibrate a moment ago.

It's never too late. Please, Sophie, for your baby's sake, take your passport and run. If you cannot escape then just say the word and we will rescue you.

Sophie read the messages with unfamiliar anger swelling inside her.

She fired a message back.

I don't need rescuing. Javier is the father of my child. I've married him.

Less than a minute later came the reply.

You don't know what he's capable of. He destroyed Benjamin and they'd been friends since they were babies. His own twin has disowned him. He is unfit to be a father. He's dangerous. He will destroy you and your baby. Let us help you.

'You look worried.'

Sophie screamed and jumped.

She had no idea how a man as large as Javier could tread so quietly that she hadn't heard him enter the bedroom.

She backed against the wall and pressed the phone to her chest, an automatic action, which caused him to narrow his eyes.

'Something I should know about?' he asked when the only sound coming from her was ragged breaths.

She wanted to smile and say there was nothing wrong but knew her scarlet cheeks would betray the lie.

He treaded slowly towards her with his hand extended. 'Give me the phone.'

She shook her head and whispered, 'You don't need to see this.'

He really did not need to see those messages.

'I will be the judge of that.'

He stood before her, the expression in his eyes clearly stating she would be going nowhere until she gave him her phone.

She dropped it into his hand, her heart dropping to her feet with it. If she didn't let him read them it would fester in him. He might make assumptions that were even worse.

They needed to build trust between them, which meant openness and honesty.

But she wished he wouldn't read them.

By no stretch of the imagination could Javier be described as an angel but those were messages no one should have to read about themselves.

He scrolled through them, emotionless.

After an age had passed he looked back at her, a pulse throbbing in his temples. 'Do you believe yourself to be in danger from me?'

She didn't have to think twice about her answer. 'No.'

He was dangerous, that she did believe. Javier was a man you crossed at your peril. Cross him and he would strike back twice as hard with all the force at his disposal.

His chest rose as he breathed deeply. 'Maybe you should believe it.'

'And maybe you should trust that if I thought you were a danger to me or our child I would never have exchanged vows with you. I would have kept our baby a secret from you.'

Silence stretched between them and with it a tension, there in the air they breathed, thickening as it wrapped its tentacles around them.

The intensity of his stare upon her, the swirling shapes forming and darkening the light of his eyes…

She had never seen it before. Not even when he'd leaned in to kiss her…

Low in her belly a heat began to grow. It spread into her veins and down into her bones, then pulsed to cover her skin with warm, darting tingles.

His breathing deepened visibly but still he didn't speak, his jaw clenched too tightly for words.

The ache she carried with her intensified and suddenly Sophie knew, as she knew he would never hurt her, that he would never make the first move to touch her. She didn't know why but she knew it to be true.

If she wanted their marriage to be a true one and not a piece of paper she had to be the one to instigate it.

Gathering all her courage, she slowly turned her back to him and tried to breathe through the thuds of her heart. 'Could you undo my dress for me, please?'

There was a long pause.

'Please? I can't reach.'

She closed her eyes and held her breath.

The hairs on the nape of her neck lifted and her skin warmed as he stepped to her.

At the first touch of his fingers to her spine the breath she'd been holding escaped.

Javier fought to keep his mind detached from what his fingers were doing.

He found the top button, a tiny, delicate creation, and, careful not to touch her milky skin, undid it.

Then he unbuttoned the one below and the one below that, not allowing even a breath of air into his lungs as he worked.

When he reached the final button at the base of her spine, he stepped back and cleared his throat. 'You're done.'

Was that *his* voice sounding so thick?

'Thank you,' she murmured.

About to make his excuses and leave the room, she turned back around and faced him.

Her eyes were a darker shade of blue than he had ever seen.

The lump that he'd only just cleared from his throat returned.

Her eyes not leaving his, she took the top of one lace sleeve between her fingers and slowly slid it down her arm, then did the same with the other.

When both arms were free, she pulled the dress down to her waist, pinched a hidden zipper at the side and pulled that down too, then let the dress fall to her feet.

Javier tried to force his feet to move, to leave this room and all the danger charging in the electricity Sophie was creating, but they refused to obey.

And now she straightened, those beautiful eyes still on him, not a single word uttered from the rosebud lips, wearing only a lacy white bra and matching knickers, and the most incredible high, lace-covered white shoes.

His mouth ran dry.

Suddenly he no longer fought his feet to move. Now he was fighting his heart's erratic rhythm and his fingers' itchy determination to touch the silky white skin.

Hermosa. That was what Sophie was. Beautiful.

He'd noticed the changes their child was making to her body earlier but seeing it like this now, in the flesh, sucked all the air from him.

In a little under three months her athletic femininity had softened. The small breasts his hands had covered so thrillingly had grown, the flat stomach now softly rounded, her narrow hips wider. She was like a flower coming into bloom and there was not a single part of him that did not ache to see it.

Still looking at him with that open yet endearingly shy expression, she raised a hand to her hair and pulled a long pin out of it. She cast the pin aside as the blonde tresses fell down.

Heavy beats sounded around the room like a drum was playing in it.

And then he realised the beats were coming from inside him, from the rapid tattoo of his heart.

The bra was the next item to be removed.

Now he could hear his breaths too as he forced air in and out through his nose.

Her bare breasts jutted out, ripe, beautiful and more tempting than the apple in the Garden of Eden.

Then she put her hands to the band of her knickers and down they went too. When she stepped out of them, she stepped out of the shoes, naked from head to toe, every trembling part exquisite.

Her shoulders rose as she took a long breath, then put one foot in front of the other to stand close enough that the scented heat of her skin landed like a heady punch to his senses.

She placed a hand on his shoulder. Raising herself onto her tiptoes, she grazed the lightest of kisses to his mouth, then pulled back enough to stare into his eyes, a plea resonating from hers.

As if she had willed it—there was no conscious thought from himself in the action—his hand reached forward to rest on her hip. With no conscious thought from himself, his fingers kneaded into the warm satin skin.

All week he'd resisted the walking temptation that was Sophie, the consequences of their one coupling there in every step and every breath she took.

The detachment he'd been waiting for before making love to her had never felt so far away.

But his need for her had never been so great.

Dios, his skin burned through his shirt under the gentle weight of her hand on his shoulder.

He snatched at her hand and covered it tightly. 'Do not expect more than I can give you, *carina*.' He had to drag the warning from his tongue but he had to make her understand.

If any other woman had offered herself to him like this he would already have taken her but this was no ordinary woman and it wasn't just because she carried his child.

Sophie was like no one he'd ever known before.

Her face drew closer to his. Her lips parted, brushing

against his like a sigh. The sweetness of her breath mingled with his as she whispered, 'I want no more than you can give.'

His heavy heart lightened although the beats continued to thump against his ribs.

The relief when Javier returned the pressure of her lips was so immense Sophie could have wept.

She'd never known she possessed the courage she'd found to strip completely naked for him. Nudity was nothing to a ballerina but this was different.

This was her opening herself to him and the very real danger of his rejection but she had known she had to keep going, known that Javier had the strength of mind and the willpower to lie beside her every night for the rest of their lives without making a move on her, and now she understood why.

He did not trust her to take him at his word that their marriage could never be about emotions.

In his own way he was trying to protect her.

She did not need protecting. Once, she'd had romantic dreams and ideals about this man but her eyes had been opened. To fall for him would be to have her heart broken.

But her desire for him had never dimmed. This was the man she had taken one look at and felt something inside her move as it had never moved before. Javier had awoken something in her. When he'd made love to her, that awakening had become a life force that refused to go back to sleep.

She didn't want it to go back to sleep. She wanted this. All of this.

When the hand holding her hip slid round her waist and splayed on her back, the little control she had was lost. Suddenly it was Javier setting the pace, kissing her, sweeping his tongue into her mouth and filling her with his dark taste, holding her so securely that when her knees weakened at this wonderful assault on her senses there was no danger of her falling.

Such wonderful, heady kisses, deepening, tongues entwined, lips moving in a dance of their own creation, sensation fizzing through her all the way to the fingertips of her arms that looped around his neck.

Her mind closed to everything but Javier.

She shivered to feel his fingers spear her hair and then his mouth caressed over her cheek and dipped down to her neck, the stubble on his jaw rubbing against flesh she'd never known could be so sensitive.

And then she was lifted off her feet, her stomach swooping with the unexpected motion, and carried effortlessly to the bed she'd been losing hope would ever be used for anything but sleeping.

He laid her down with a gentleness that belied his strength and knelt beside her, upright, magnificent. Beautiful.

Nostrils flaring, he gazed down at her through his hooded eyes, deftly unbuttoned his shirt and threw it onto the floor.

Her heart expanded as she drank in the rugged hardness of his torso. Javier was the epitome of masculine. Whorls of dark hair covered his darkly tanned, muscular chest and thickened over the flat plane of his abdomen where his strong hands were pulling apart his belt.

Her own abdomen contracted and filled with fresh heat that burned like molten liquid inside her.

There was such sensuality to his movements and such arrogant confidence too as, his eyes not leaving hers, he pushed his trousers down and revealed the erection she'd touched and had buried deep inside her but had never looked at.

Everything inside her seemed to melt into a puddle.

With a sigh that seemed to come from her very soul,

Sophie watched him rid himself of the last of his clothing and then he was as naked as she, but dark where she was light, hard where she was soft…

Those whirling eyes were devouring her in the same way hers devoured him, sweeping over every inch of her naked form.

For years Sophie had worked hard sculpting her body to be the best it could be. It had never been enough. She had never been the best.

Pregnancy had liberated her in so many ways, more than she could ever have expected, and now, for the first time in her life, under the weight of Javier's sensuous stare, she felt beautiful.

She felt like a woman.

It came to her then that she'd been waiting her entire life to feel this way but then the thought was swept away before it had fully formed as he leaned down and set her mouth on fire with his kisses all over again.

She closed her eyes and embraced it, wrapped her arms around his neck to embrace him.

And then he made his way down her body to kiss her in places even fellow dancers' eyes had never seen.

Over her swollen, sensitive breasts, kneading them, caressing them, so close to her he would be able to see and hear the jagged beats of her heart. Over her thickened stomach, a circle around her belly button, his tongue and mouth leaving trails of fire in their wake. He kissed and touched her everywhere with such expert precision that when he parted her legs to bury his face into her pubis her eyes flew open and, chest shuddering, she was pulled back to reality.

Sophie stared at the ceiling, a feeling rushing through her that she was part of a game that involved painting by numbers.

She was in danger of losing her mind but from Javier there was no sound other than his lips against her flesh.

The thought dissolved when his tongue flickered against her most feminine nub and then she did lose her mind.

Squeezing her eyes back shut, she submitted to the pleasure he was evoking in her, submitted to the pulses thickening and swelling deep inside her and let go, letting him take her high into a land where nothing but white light shone.

Only once the sensations had abated did he move back up her body and position himself between her legs.

Again came the distant thought that this was painting by numbers for him.

There was no danger of Javier losing his control.

He was going through the motions.

He had given her pleasure and now it was his turn.

But, again, the thoughts were pushed away as he covered her with his glorious body and drove himself deep inside her, filling her so completely that she was helpless to stop the cry that flew from her mouth at the sudden drive of pleasure.

Javier adjusted himself so his elbows lay by her shoulders and began to move, concentrating hard as he thrust deeply into her.

He had to keep his concentration.

Otherwise…

A black void beckoned him. It was a void falsely dressed in sunlight, a trick, a mirage, a promise of…something beautiful but which was a lie. It was a void with razor-sharp teeth hidden beneath its seductive exterior.

He *had* to concentrate.

He wanted Sophie to have the pleasure. All of it belonged to her. He would take his too but his would be the release of sex. He would not allow it to be anything more. He could not.

And so he gritted his teeth and kept his head exactly where he needed it to be and let Sophie's reactions guide him.

Dios, she was so hot and tight around him…

Do not let go.

Hold on. Keep your head. Close your senses to the woman lying beneath you. This was only normal pleasure, nothing special. It meant nothing.

Nothing at all.

His resolve teetered when her fingers burrowed into his hair and he found her wide-eyed stare, full of wonder, piercing straight through him.

He shifted his position slightly and upped the pace, then screwed his eyes tightly shut and banished the sight of her open-mouthed sighs from his retinas.

But he couldn't banish the sighs from his ears. They deepened, becoming moans. The hand tracing marks up and down his back tightened around him, the fingers burrowed in his hair grabbing as she crushed herself to him, limbs wrapped tightly around him as if she were melding herself to become a part of him.

He felt her climax as powerfully as if it belonged to him. It gripped him and pulled at him, winding him tighter and tighter…

The sensations were…

Incredible.

Dios, this was like nothing he had ever felt before, stronger and deeper than even their first time together.

He was starting to float, the void right there before him, ready to swallow him into its dangerous depths…

Right before he could fall into it, sanity found its way to him. Clenching his jaw so tightly that only the slightest extra pressure would see it snap, Javier turned his face from Sophie and forced his eyes open.

His gaze burning a hole in the wall, his attention

wrenched far from the woman coming undone in his arms, he accepted the rush of his own, determinedly unremarkable release.

It was over.

When he was certain Sophie had taken all the pleasure she could, he let out a breath and rolled off her onto his back.

He swallowed hard, his gaze now fixed on the ceiling, and braced himself for her to say something.

For a long period of time the only sounds in his bedroom were their breaths, both ragged.

There was light movement beside him, the shifting of air...

He turned his head to see her slip into the bathroom.

She locked the door behind her.

CHAPTER SEVEN

SOPHIE SOAKED IN the bath she'd rerun for herself until the water went cold and her toes had turned into prunes.

She did not want to go back into the bedroom and face Javier's cold shoulder.

What they had shared had been wonderful. It had also been awful.

His distance had made it awful.

Where she should be bathing in a heady glow at all the wonderful sensations and feelings that had erupted in her, all she wanted was to crawl under a rock and bawl her eyes out.

Javier had committed himself with his body but the part that really mattered, the heartfelt connection she hadn't re-alised she craved until it had been denied her, had not been there and that had been deliberate, she was certain of it.

She did not deny that he'd been generous in his attention to her. In that respect it had been glorious but she could savour none of it because it all felt tainted.

Would he have held back so absolutely from Freya…?

She pulled at her hair and stifled a scream.

Comparing herself would do her no favours. Freya was incomparable. She always had been.

After she'd brushed her teeth and pulled her old, com-fortable pyjamas on, Sophie felt better in herself, better enough to deal with the silence that would be waiting for her in the bedroom.

She rubbed her stomach and made a promise to their child that she would not admit defeat. They'd been married only half a day!

She was expecting too much from him.

She was suffering a severe case of reality trumping expectations when she should be rejoicing that she'd broken enough of his barriers for him to share their bed as it should be shared, not whinging that he hadn't stared deep into her eyes and declared his undying love.

Whoa!

Her hand was on the door as that thought went through her head.

She walked back to the small shaving mirror and stared at her reflection sternly.

Stop thinking, she told it. *You knew the man you were committing to was an emotionless control freak, so stop being surprised when he acts like an emotionless control freak and don't give even a passing thought to love. It's not going to happen. Javier's incapable of love and you're not stupid enough to fall for the man who threw you out of his home after taking your virginity and then forgot all about you.*

Rolling her shoulders, Sophie tucked her hair behind her ears and walked back into the bedroom.

Her resolution almost faltered to find the bedside light still on and Javier lying in bed, an arm crooked on the pillow above his head, the sheets pulled up to his waist.

His eyes were open.

He didn't say anything, just watched her pad to the bed.

She was glad of her pyjamas. It meant he couldn't see her shaking knees.

She climbed onto the bed and crossed her legs, facing him.

It warmed her that his returning stare was curious rather than hostile or indifferent.

A bubble of laughter flew up her throat that she only just managed to stop from escaping, but it wasn't the laughter of amusement, only the laughter of sadness.

She guessed he'd prepared himself for histrionics from her.

Did her calmness relieve or disappoint him?

She pulled at a loose thread at the ankle of her pyjama bottoms and, in as casual a tone as she could muster, asked, 'What happened with Benjamin to make him hate you so much?'

His features darkened, just as she'd known they would.

This was a conversation they needed to have. Why not have it now, when they were both awake and alone?

Better to talk than lie in silence with only her thoughts.

'That is none of your business.'

She'd expected the brusqueness of his reply. 'I'm your wife. Like it or not, that means your business is now my business.'

He laughed mirthlessly. 'That didn't take long.'

'What didn't?'

'For you to assert your wifely rights.'

'It's going to come out, you know that, surely? The world knows you and Luis took out an injunction on Benjamin and sooner or later some journalist or other will find the details and publish them.'

'Nothing can be published. The injunction prevents it.'

'It can in America. Do you want me to hear it from the press or from yourself? Or shall I ask Freya?'

'You are to have nothing to do with her.'

'Javier...' She sighed at his bullishness. 'Freya's the reason I'm asking you this. You read the messages she sent me. Whatever she believes you did, she hates you for it.

Whatever went wrong between you and Benjamin, I would rather hear your side first before anyone else's.'

'My *side*?' he asked in that all too familiar dangerous tone.

'It will be different from theirs because you will see things from your own perspective. I reached out to her today because Freya's my oldest friend and I didn't want her to learn about our marriage from anyone but me. She's found happiness with Benjamin and I am very happy for them but my loyalty now belongs to you.'

'That does not say much about your loyalty if it is so easily transferred.'

'Freya has had my loyalty and friendship since we were eleven years old. She will always be my best friend but I did not take our vows lightly. You're my husband. You're the father of my child. That means everything and if your vows meant anything then you have to start trusting me. I'm not your enemy, Javier.'

Trust her? As if he would trust anyone ever again.

But there was something in the softness in those pale blue eyes and the soothing melodiousness of her voice that made Javier wish...

In that softly thickening belly lay his child.

He had observed Sophie with her parents that day and seen the bond she had with them. She had given up the support she would undoubtedly have received from them throughout the pregnancy and birth to be with him. She had signed the iron contract he'd drawn up that stated exactly what she'd suggested: that in the event of them divorcing she would be entitled to a home in Madrid and that they would share custody of any children they had.

She had read it thoroughly in front of him, asked for a pen and signed it. She hadn't argued any of it. She had signed it knowing she would get nothing else from him.

He'd been testing her. He'd been prepared to give her much more but she hadn't asked.

Damn Freya to hell for trying to poison her against him. He had been straight down the line with Freya and she repaid him like this?

He had to give Sophie credit for not simply calling Freya and demanding the details.

If she was prepared to hear him out then he could meet her halfway.

'Benjamin thinks Luis and I owe him two hundred and twenty-five million euros in profit from the Tour Mont Blanc project,' he said heavily. 'When a judge threw his case out of court, he refused to accept it. He stole Freya from me in revenge.'

'Why did he refuse to accept it?'

'He won't accept responsibility for his own actions. He didn't read the contract. If he had read it he would have seen his share of the profit had been changed from twenty per cent to five per cent. That was on the advice of our lawyer.'

She didn't say anything for the longest time. 'They say money is the root of all evil and it really is.'

'They are wrong. Evil is the root of all evil.' His father had been evil. He'd been charming when he'd wanted to be but his malevolence had never been far from the surface.

'But you were friends with Benjamin since you were babies. All those years and all those memories thrown away for cash.' She shrugged and gave a sad smile.

'Sentimentality does not pay the bills,' he told her roughly.

His and Luis's friendship with Benjamin had been foisted on them by their mothers. The two women had deliberately conceived their children at the same time so they could raise them together. Benjamin's mother had been Javier's mother's personal costume maker; mother and son accompanying them on all Clara's tours around the world, the boys expected to get along and play together.

'I get that,' Sophie said with a sigh, 'but…'

'If you show weakness in life then people learn they can walk all over you.'

'But he was your friend. Why didn't he read the contract? Didn't he know the terms had been changed?'

'You would have to ask him that.'

'I'm asking you. You're the one who took the injunction out.'

'We took it because he'd become emotional and unpredictable and would not listen to reason. He threatened to destroy us.'

He remembered clearly Benjamin's shouted threats that had ricocheted like a bullet in the courtroom and the rage on his face.

Javier and Luis had filed the injunction immediately, both certain Benjamin's threats would be acted on and that the consequences would be disastrous for them.

If the world believed the Casillas brothers could rip off their closest friend, who would ever trust them in business again?

Sophie winced and drew her knees up to her chest, wrapping her arms around them. 'Where did all his anger come from? Please, don't think I'm not listening, I'm just trying to understand. Freya had no fears about marrying you even though you have a fearsome reputation and I'm trying to understand why her opinion towards you has shifted so completely.'

'Benjamin has poisoned her towards me.' And if he and Luis hadn't slapped the injunction to stop him talking about the soured business deal he would have poisoned the world against them too. Benjamin's actions in stealing Freya had almost succeeded in doing that for him but they had ridden the storm of malicious press as a united force, right until Luis had turned his back on thirty-five years of brotherhood to be with Benjamin's sister.

Chloe Guillem had stolen Luis's loyalty in a way her brother had never been able to do.

The destruction of the friendship lay not at the feet of the Casillas brothers. They hadn't put a gun to Benjamin's forehead and made him sign. He'd had five hours to read the contract and get back to them if the terms were not to his liking and, sure, it had been argued in court, by Benjamin, that they had known he'd been preoccupied that day but, as Javier had counter-argued, that meant Benjamin should have given the contract to his lawyer to read for him. That was what lawyers were for.

'Freya knows her own mind,' Sophie stated with certainty. 'She never listens to gossip.'

'If you think so much of her opinion then why are you still here?' he bit back.

'She's just being protective.'

'Why? Does she not think you know *your* own mind?'

'No, it's just the nature of our friendship. We've looked out for each other since ballet school.'

Grabbing at the change of direction in a conversation that was making his brain burn and his skin feel as if it had needles poking in it, Javier sat up. 'You two are an unlikely friendship.'

Freya was cold and driven; Sophie warm and open.

She tightened her hold around her knees. 'I know, but the differences weren't so pronounced when we were kids. She was amazingly talented, even back then, and it was obvious to everyone that she was a dancer who would set the world alight but when we first met she was incredibly shy and insecure. She comes across as cold but that's because she had to be to get through school. She was really badly bullied, especially that first term.'

'Were you a part of it?'

But he knew the answer to that before she shook her head in denial.

He doubted Sophie was capable of bullying a dormouse.

'God no. I just felt sorry for her. She was this scared little thing, away from home for the first time, from a poor background when everyone else came from families with money. She was admitted on a full scholarship, which was incredibly rare—I mean, I only got in because my parents paid the fees.'

'Your family has money?' Her parents didn't have the moneyed air about them that most rich people had.

'Not as much as most of the other girls had but my parents would have lived in a shed if it meant me going to ballet school. Luckily it didn't come to that,' she added, rubbing her chin on her knee.

'You weren't scared, being away from home yourself?'

'I'd already built a resilience. Freya had to build hers. She had the talent—my God, did she have the talent—but it was a tough time for her. The other girls hated her. It was jealousy, pure and simple.'

'You were not jealous yourself?'

'I was definitely envious but not jealous.'

'Is there a difference?' Javier remembered his mother once telling him sharply to stop being jealous of Luis and Benjamin's friendship when she'd caught him sitting on his own, scowling as he'd watched them plot ways to put itching powder in the *corps de ballet* costumes.

She hadn't understood that he was watching over Luis, ready to step in if things went too far.

Benjamin had brought Luis's worst instincts out in him. They'd egged each other on in their troublemaking, leaving Javier to cover for their messes as best he could, terrified his father would hear and mete out punishment.

Their father had needed little excuse to punish Luis.

Had Javier been jealous of Luis and Benjamin's friendship as his mother had accused?

No, he assured himself. He'd been looking out for his brother.

Every mark their father had made on Luis's body Javier had felt as if it had been delivered on his own skin.

'Sure there's a difference,' she answered with a rueful smile. 'I would have loved to dance as well as Freya did but I would never hate her for it. I felt so sorry for her and the way those mean girls treated her that I wanted to protect her. I became her shadow. The poor thing couldn't get rid of me.'

'You weren't worried they would turn their cruelty on you?'

'It didn't cross my mind and I wouldn't have cared if they did. I could never sit back and watch someone suffer if it was in my power to help them.'

'What are you, some kind of saint?'

Her answering laugh was as mocking as his words. 'Hardly.'

Maybe not a saint, he thought, gazing at her, noting for the first time that she had not met his eyes once since getting on the bed, but there was an inherent goodness about his new wife.

His heart thumped loudly against his ribcage as the strangest impulse to gather this beautiful, compassionate creature into his arms filled him.

He closed his eyes and breathed deeply, willing the impulse away, not knowing where it had come from, just knowing that nothing good could come from it, not for her, pampered and cosseted all her life as she had been.

It was easy to be a good person, he thought scathingly, when you'd known nothing but love and indulgence in your life.

What troubles had his wife had? Not being the best

dancer in the school was the extent of it and that wasn't something that had bothered her, strange though the concept of a professional dancer happy to settle for being less than the best was to him. Even their unplanned baby she considered to be a blessing.

The harsh, cruel realities of the world had never touched Sophie on a personal level. She had only ever observed it, had no concept of what it was like to feel it and live it.

He quite understood why Freya had felt compelled to warn her of him. Look at her, sitting there, not caring of the danger she was in just to share a bed with him.

She wanted to know why Freya and Benjamin hated him so much? He would tell her. Let her eyes be opened by the truth.

'Benjamin hates us because we approached him for the investment in the Tour Mont Blanc project on the day his mother's cancer was diagnosed as terminal.'

Now her eyes did rise to meet his.

'He doesn't just believe we ripped him off but believes we took advantage of him,' he added for good measure.

'And did you?' she asked with a whisper.

'We did not rip him off.' Of that he was vehement.

'What about taking advantage of him? Did you?'

'Not deliberately. We'd paid the seller of the land a huge deposit. He then came to us and gave us twenty hours to pay the remainder or he would sell to another interested buyer. We didn't have the ready cash for it, so we asked Benjamin if he wanted to invest. Neither Luis nor myself were aware that Benjamin had just received that diagnosis. He'd been minutes from calling us with the news. His mother had been best friends with our mother.'

Their friendship had seen the two women raise their children as family. When Javier and Luis's mother had been killed, Louise Guillem had been the one to break the news to them. Afterwards, she had taken them under her wing as much as she could.

Javier had felt little in the way of emotion since his mother's death but when he'd carried Louise's coffin he'd felt the weight in his heart as on his shoulder.

'He signed the contract that same day?' she asked.

'Yes.'

'Thinking he would receive twenty per cent of the profit?'

'Yes. I didn't know he hadn't read it until after it was signed.'

'You didn't warn him?'

'Why should I have done? I thought he would read it or get his lawyer to.'

'That's cold.'

'Just starting to realise that, are you?' he mocked. Let her see the truth because so far she'd seemed determined to keep herself blind. 'Business is business. He didn't have to say yes to the investment.'

'So you did take advantage of him.'

'Not initially and not deliberately. When I realised he hadn't read the contract my feelings on the matter were simple; it was his own fault. It was business, not personal.'

'But Benjamin doesn't see it like that,' she supposed, rightly. 'And I would guess that he wouldn't have entertained the idea of doing any business that day if it hadn't been you and your brother doing the asking.'

'Maybe he wouldn't have but he did. Do not forget, Benjamin made seventy-five million euros in profit on that investment. He has been handsomely rewarded.'

'But not as handsomely rewarded as he'd thought he would be.'

'If he'd read the contract he would have seen the terms had been changed. If he'd been unhappy about that he could have negotiated.'

'If you didn't warn him the terms had changed he didn't know to read it. He trusted you.'

The stab in his guts at this truth hit him hard.

He refused to let it take hold, just as he'd resisted it for seven years.

He allowed no room for sentimentality in his life, never mind his business, and he would not allow Sophie's soft chastisement to breach that.

Throwing the covers off, Javier climbed out of bed and grabbed his boxer shorts off the floor. 'Trust should not have come into it. Not with business. I would never sign a contract without reading it first, no matter who presented it to me.'

'You were not in his shoes. Couldn't you have made an allowance on this occasion? For his state of mind about his mother? Torn the contract up and renegotiated?'

'No one made allowances for me after my father killed my mother.'

Even under the dim hue of the bedside light he saw her face drain of colour.

Good. She needed to wake up to the truth.

He was his father's son, his father's favourite, his father's mirror image inside *and* out.

Shaking his trousers out first, he pulled them up. 'Luis and I had to fight to get the business world to take us seriously, to get credit, to get investment…we've had to fight for everything. We live with the legacy of our mother's death every day of our lives and if that has made me cold and ruthless then so be it. It's called survival, something you with your unicorn-and-rainbow-filled childhood know nothing about. I warned you of the man I am, so go ahead, judge me and condemn me, but understand your condemnation means nothing to me.'

Turning his back on Sophie's white, shocked face, he stormed out of the bedroom and headed down to the basement, to his gym, intent on nothing more than pounding the crap out of his punching bag.

Dios, everything inside him felt as if it were being ripped in a hundred different directions by vicious hands.

She had wanted the truth and he'd given it to her.

He'd warned her before they married. He'd kept his distance since she'd moved in. He'd arranged their wedding to be as sparse as it could be. He'd made love to her with a detachment that had been brutal but none of it had been enough.

Sophie saw the world through eyes set to a different filter from his own.

Listening to her relate how she'd willingly put herself in the bullies' firing line to protect and support Freya and stop her feeling alone had hit a strong nerve in him.

She touched him in ways that were dangerous and Freya had been completely right that she needed protecting from him.

He was his father's son!

He'd wanted her to see him for who he truly was, see the monster that lived inside him, never have her rest her hands on him and look at him with those eyes in the way she had again.

He never again wanted to look into her eyes and feel as if she were reaching down into his soul…

He sensed rather than heard movement behind him.

Lowering his hands from the punching bag he'd been battering, he turned.

Sophie was standing in the doorway, a glass of water in her hand and an apprehensive look on her face.

CHAPTER EIGHT

In that moment, standing in the doorway of Javier's gym, Sophie glimpsed the anger and pain resonating from his eyes and knew she had made the right decision to come to him.

For the second time in one night she had found courage she'd never known she possessed.

His revelations about his treatment of Benjamin had shocked her to her core but not, she suspected, for the reasons he'd wanted her to be shocked.

There had been fleeting remorse when she had questioned him about the contract. Only fleeting, but she had seen it.

Javier wanted her to hate him, she'd realised as she'd sat frozen on the empty bed.

He hated himself.

When he'd looked at her and made the cutting comment about his father killing his mother…

It had been a veiled warning to her that had suddenly made sense of everything: his distance, his solitary life, his brusqueness…

Javier had built the steel heart to protect himself, believing he was protecting others from himself.

Was it coincidence that he didn't drink?

His father had been a violent alcoholic whose drunken outbursts and hair-trigger temper had seen an early, ignominious end to his dance career.

By contrast, his mother's career had soared. Today, over twenty years after her death, she was still regarded as one the most dazzling ballerinas to have graced the world's stages.

Clara Casillas's dazzling star had been snuffed out when her husband had locked her in her dressing room after she'd performed in *Romeo & Juliet* and strangled her with his bare hands. Javier and his twin had been thirteen.

What kind of life had they had with a father like that, even before he'd so cruelly taken their mother's life?

It twisted her heart to imagine the cruelty Javier had been on the receiving end of and witness to.

His heart had been so damaged that he'd remorselessly used his oldest friend to his own advantage and cut his own twin from his life.

If she had any sense she would cut and run, flee from this beautiful villa and keep running as far as she could from him.

But how could she do that and live with her conscience?

Javier was trying to protect her from himself. That in itself proved the father of her child was not irredeemable.

Buried deep inside him was a good man fighting to get out.

And here, in his private gym, he'd been fighting his demons with a punching bag, his bare torso glistening with perspiration, evidence of the exertion he'd used.

He would never use her or any other person as his punching bag. That was a certainty she felt right in her marrow.

She was not ready to wave the white flag.

She stepped over to him.

'I thought you might be thirsty,' she said softly, holding the glass out.

His throat moved.

The fleshy lips pulled into a tight line before he took

the glass from her and, his eyes holding hers, drank the water in four huge swallows.

The knuckles holding the glass were red.

'Shouldn't you wear boxing gloves?'

His shoulders rose in a shrug, the light brown eyes still not moving from hers.

She longed to touch him. She longed to gather this great bear of a man into her arms and caress all the demons out of him. To make love to him with his eyes holding hers. To free him.

She settled on removing the glass from his hand, putting it on the ledge beside her and taking hold of his hand to gently rub the raw knuckles.

The tension coming from his unresponsive fingers made her want to cry.

She sighed. 'I'm sorry for pushing things but, Javier, please, try not to see me as your enemy or as some fragile creature who needs protecting from you. I'm tougher than you think and you're not going to scare me away. It's not going to be easy but we *can* make our marriage work but only if you meet me halfway. I'll stop pushing for more than you can give if you stop pushing me away at every turn. How does that sound?'

The hand she held flexed imperceptibly. Slowly, as if they were being wound by an old unused lever, his fingers closed around hers before his other hand buried into her hair and he brought his forehead down to rest against hers.

His features were taut as his eyes bore into hers. 'I am afraid I will hurt you.'

The raw honesty in his voice punctured her heart.

Sophie swallowed back all the emotions racing up her throat and rested her palm against his cheek. 'The only way you can hurt me is if you don't give us the chance our child deserves.'

That was who she was fighting for. Their innocent child.

'That is not the kind of hurt I am talking about.'

'I know.' She brushed her lips to his. 'And I know you will never hurt me or our baby in the way you mean.'

'How can you be so certain?'

'Because I would feel it.'

'Feelings cannot be trusted.'

'Sometimes feelings are all we can trust.'

The fingers gripping her hair tightened as he breathed in deeply.

It would take no effort to hurt this woman, Javier thought. No effort at all.

How could she trust he wouldn't abuse his disproportionate strength and power against her as his father had done, first to his brother, who he had revelled in abusing with the form of corporal punishment he'd malevolently deemed to be necessary and corrective, and then on that fateful night when he had used his strength as a weapon to take his mother's life?

Where did Sophie's trust come from? She must know it would take little effort for him to do serious damage to her.

It would be as easy as breaking a butterfly's wings.

Could those eyes staring so trustingly into his read the train of his thoughts?

It felt as if every organ in his body clenched, the strength enough to send a wave of nausea racing through him.

Why had the fates brought this woman of all women into his life? What cruelty had set them on this path together?

How could she put her life and trust in nothing more than a feeling?

He could not begin to comprehend it, nor comprehend why his heart hammered with such strength or why he was bringing his mouth to hers to taste those rosebud lips and the sweetness of her kisses again.

Dios, this had to stop.

Breaking the kiss, he took her face in his hands.

'I will try to meet you halfway,' he said roughly, 'but I promise nothing. I can't make promises when I don't know if I can keep them.'

'I wouldn't want to hear them if they were lies.'

'That is one promise I *can* make. I will never lie to you.'

'And I will never lie to you.'

His lips found hers again as if they had a will of their own.

Her lips returned the kiss as if she were taking the air she needed to breathe from them.

Everything about her was so soft. Her skin, her hair, her heart...

Soft, pliable and being entrusted into his large, brutal hands.

'How long are you going to be away for?' Sophie asked, making sure to keep her tone neutral.

She did not want Javier to know how much she dreaded the thought of him going away.

In the two weeks since they'd been married, it would be the first time they had slept apart.

He looked up from his phone. 'Five nights if it all goes well.'

Her spirits sank even lower.

Five nights?

When he'd casually mentioned that he'd be going on a business trip to Cape Town for a few days, she'd thought he meant two or three.

His case was already packed and in the car.

She supposed she should be grateful that he'd stayed to eat breakfast with her before leaving.

Although he hadn't said so in words, she was aware the exclusive apartment complex he intended to build in the

South African city was the first development he would be undertaking without his brother.

The pressure he was under must be horrendous.

She'd deliberately held herself back from asking too many questions about it.

They had reached an understanding on their wedding night. She was not to push too hard. He was to stop pushing her away with so much force.

So far it was, tentatively, working.

She put no pressure on him and asked nothing of him.

He ate most evening meals with her. Sometimes he even put his phone down and talked to her.

He no longer slept with his back to her.

That was the best and worst aspect of it all. Now that the genie of sex had been let out of its bottle they made love every night.

She wished they could make love more. During the long, boring days when she whiled her time away swimming either in the outdoor pool when the weather was sunny or in the indoor pool when it was a bit too chilly for her, or exploring Madrid's streets as she'd never had a chance to do before when she'd spent six days a week in a dance studio, she found her thoughts continually drifting to him.

She'd made a promise not to push him for more than he could give but as the days passed she found she wanted so much more. Sometimes the urge to call him, just to hear his voice, would overwhelm her.

And although their lovemaking was regular and frequent that magic ingredient she kept hoping for never came through. The connection she craved still wasn't there.

Javier was still holding back.

He was always considerate; on that she could not fault him. He never took his release before she found hers.

When they were done, she would lie with her head pressed against his chest, her hand in his. On paper, he was ticking all the boxes, painting in all the numbers.

She wanted more. More passion, more spontaneity, wanted to feel that he desired *her*, that he wasn't going through the expected motions with the woman he'd been forced into marrying because she carried his child. When their lovemaking was over, she longed to drape her limbs all over him, mesh herself to his skin and relish the scent of their sex that lingered in the air, but always held herself back from doing any of these things.

Javier reached for his coffee and surprised her by continuing the conversation. 'I've been thinking…'

'Oh?'

'While I'm away, you should start organising the baby's nursery.'

'Really?' she asked dubiously.

'You said only last night that you're bored.'

He'd listened to her?

It had been a passing comment made after yet another day of doing nothing useful. She might not miss dance but she missed being active and having a purpose in her life. She hadn't expected Javier to take her comment seriously.

'Don't you want to have any input with the nursery?' she asked.

'No. I'll get my PA to sort a credit card out for you today. Spend whatever you like on it—there will be no limit. It will be yours to keep.' His eyes narrowed as he contemplated her. 'I also think it's time we sorted out an allowance for you.'

'I don't need one.' If she needed money there was a petty-cash drawer in Javier's home office filled with an ever-replenishing stack of euro notes that she helped herself to at his insistence, always leaving a note of how much she'd taken and what it was for. 'It's not as if I have any bills to pay.'

'Everyone needs money to call their own. You shouldn't have to feel that you need my permission to spend money.'

'I don't feel that,' she protested.

His gaze was critical. '*Carina*, you're my wife and carrying my child. Your clothes are tight on you.'

He'd noticed?

'You will have an allowance,' he said in the tone she'd learned not to bother arguing with. 'While I'm away, I want you to go shopping and spoil yourself. If you have the time, arrange the nursery. Julio will have the names of decorators who can paint it out in whatever colour and style you want.'

'I can do it however I want?' she clarified.

His gaze was serious. 'This is your home. You need to start treating it as such.'

Everything inside her swelled so big and so quickly it felt as if she could burst.

She had never dreamed Javier would say those words to her.

'Which room shall we put the nursery in?' she asked, trying not to beam her joy at this breakthrough with him.

'There's a pair of adjoining rooms on the east wing…'

'The east wing? But that'll be too far from us.'

'The nanny will have the adjoining room.'

'What nanny?'

'The nanny *you're* going to employ.' He gave a smile that showed he thought he was being a good guy. A smile from Javier was such a rare occurrence that it momentarily startled her away from what he'd just said.

She remembered reading the clause in the old contract that had mentioned wraparound care for any child, presumably because he expected her to go back to work.

Sophie wouldn't care if she never danced again. The

thought of putting her pointe shoes on and performing made her feel all tight inside.

'We're not having a nanny,' she told him flatly, her brief moment of joy gone.

'Of course we are.'

'We are not. I'm not letting someone else raise my child.'

'A nanny would not raise it. A nanny would do the mundane chores.'

Now she was to use the tone that meant he could argue with her but she would not bend. 'This is our child and I'm not palming it off on a stranger.'

His face darkened. 'You are prepared to care for it 24/7?'

'It's called being a parent.'

'What about work? How are you going to return to dance with a baby? Do you expect to pirouette with it strapped to your back?'

'I'm not going back to the ballet.'

He stared at her as if she'd just announced an intention to fly a car to the moon. 'Why on earth not?'

'I don't want to.'

Not want to? Javier had never heard such words from a ballerina's mouth. His own mother had returned to the stage four months after giving birth to twins. To be a professional dancer meant a life of dedication and single-mindedness. His father had driven himself to alcoholic despair when the work had dried up, admittedly because of his drunken rages and violence against fellow dancers and choreographers. Javier didn't know a single ballet dancer who had quit before the age of thirty-five, most usually only doing so reluctantly when their bodies failed them, all the injuries sustained through their careers finally taking their toll.

Sophie was twenty-four. She hadn't even reached her peak.

'But you're a dancer.'

'And now I'm going to be a mother.'

'You can be both.' He shook his head, trying to comprehend this woman he was beginning to suspect he would never understand. '*Carina*, you're young. You're in excellent health. There is no reason for you not to be able to continue to dance.'

'I don't want to,' she repeated with an obstinacy he'd never seen before. 'I'm done with dance. It's not as if I was particularly good at it.'

'What are you talking about?'

'I only got into ballet school because my parents paid the full fees.'

'Did you not have to audition?'

'Well…yes, but my parents still had to pay. I'm not saying I'm a bad dancer but I'm never going to be the best. I only got the job with your ballet company because Freya put a good word in for me.'

'Rubbish.'

'It isn't rubbish…'

'Compania de Ballet de Casillas does not employ second-rate dancers. I should know; it's my company. You think anyone would dare go above my wishes for only the best to be employed?'

She gaped, a crease forming in her brow. Then she tucked a lock of hair behind her ear and grimaced. 'It doesn't matter.'

'It does. You're a dancer. You're an excellent dancer. It's in your blood.'

'It isn't,' she insisted. 'I love the ballet but… I'd been thinking of quitting before I joined your company. I think I would have done if Freya hadn't needed me here. She was having a hard time, really struggling with being so far from her mum—you know how ill she is—and I wanted to support her. Just be there when she needed a shoulder to cry on.'

'You were already thinking of quitting?'

She nodded, a wistful look on her face. 'I love the ballet, I really do, but dancing was never... My heart was never in it. It was not what I wanted to do in my life.'

'What did you want to do?'

'I wanted to be a vet.'

'A *vet*?'

His wife, a professional ballerina, who'd dedicated her life to dance had never wanted to do it. She'd wanted to be a vet.

He could hardly wrap his brain around the notion.

He thought back to their wedding night and her comment that her parents would have lived in a shed if it had meant Sophie getting into ballet school. At the time he'd treated it like a throwaway comment but now it began to resonate... Had Sophie spent her life working for a dream that wasn't her own?

What kind of a person did *that*?

The answer stared back at him. His wife. The only person in the world who he suspected was capable of such self-sacrifice.

Before he could question her further his phone buzzed. Catching the time on it, Javier blinked and hauled himself to his feet. 'I have to go. We'll finish this conversation when I get home.'

Downing the last of his coffee, he contemplated Sophie one last time.

It suddenly came to him that he wouldn't see her for another five days.

'Call me if you need anything.'

She nodded but the easy smile that was usually never far from her lips didn't appear.

Was she angry at him for giving his opinion on her career?

He didn't have time to worry about that now. He had a flight slot to fill.

Taking hold of his briefcase, he walked to the dining-room door.

'Have a safe trip,' she called to his retreating back. 'Please call or message to let me know you've got there safely.'

He took one last look at her.

'I will,' he promised.

Now she did smile but nowhere near enough for it to reach her sad eyes.

As his driver steered them out of the electric gates, Javier put his head back and closed his eyes with a sigh.

Leaving his home had never felt like a wrench before.

Whoever had coined the term 'retail therapy' could not know how right they had been.

Sophie had prevented herself bursting into tears at Javier's leaving by a thread.

He wouldn't have wanted to see her cry. It would probably have repelled him.

She didn't understand why his leaving left her feeling so heavy and wretched. They were hardly in the throes of a traditional honeymoon period. They hadn't even *had* a honeymoon!

An hour after he'd left, his PA had turned up at the villa with a credit card for her.

By what magic or trickery Javier had made it happen so quickly she could not begin to guess but it had lifted the weight off her considerably and brought a genuine smile to her face.

He'd thought of her. He'd flexed his muscles for *her* and made the impossible happen. For her.

The minute Michael, his driver, had got back from the airport she'd coerced him into taking her shopping.

She had an unlimited credit card, a nursery to fill and prepare, and a new dressing room of clothes for herself to get. Javier's observation that her clothes were getting tight had been correct. Only four months pregnant, she wasn't yet large enough for maternity wear but clothing she could breathe in easily would be welcome.

So she'd hit the shopping district she remembered exploring once with Freya, when neither of them had had the funds to do more than window-shop: Salamanca.

From there she had shopped until her feet ached, stopping only for a light lunch in a pretty little café along the Calle de Serrano.

Now she sat in the back of Javier's car, imagining the furniture she would have in their child's nursery, exhausted but happier than she had felt in months.

Javier had gone away but he had left with them in as good a state as they could be. Their marriage wasn't perfect but for the first time she really felt they were making headway.

He'd told her to treat his house as her home.

The car stopped for the electric gates to open and welcome them home.

Resting her head to the window, she noticed a tiny black bundle on the kerb.

She squinted her eyes to peer closer.

The tiny bundle made the tiniest of movements.

'Stop!' Sophie screeched before Michael could start the car again.

Unclipping her seat belt, she opened the passenger door, jumped out and hurried to see what she hoped with all her heart she was wrong about.

She wasn't wrong. The tiny black bundle was a puppy.

She crouched down next to it and put a tentative hand to its neck.

It opened its eyes and whimpered.

That was when she saw the blood and burst into tears.

CHAPTER NINE

JAVIER CLIMBED THE stairs and followed the scent of fresh paint to the room next to his.

He stepped inside it and stared around in wonder, his heart fit to burst.

'What do you think?'

He turned to find Sophie behind him, dressed in a black jersey dress that fell to her knees and covered the belly and breasts that both seemed to have grown in his absence. It would not be long, he guessed, before she would be obviously pregnant.

She looked more beautiful than ever. His bursting heart managed to expand some more.

For the longest time neither of them spoke.

Five days away from her…

He had never thought time could drag so much.

He'd expected to be relieved to have a bed to himself again.

He had not expected to find the nights so empty without her.

'You did this?' he asked.

The walls had been painted the palest yellow and covered with a hand-painted mural of white clouds and colourful smiling teddy bears.

She smiled, a wide, sweet grin that pierced straight into his chest. 'I hired a local artist to do it. I discovered her at a plaza near Calle de Serrano and offered her an obscene amount of your cash for her to drop all her other commissions and do it immediately.' Then the smile dimmed a little. 'I was hoping to warn you before you saw the room.'

'Warn me that you've turned the room next to ours into a nursery rather than the room on the east wing that I said should be used?'

She nodded and rubbed her belly. 'Even if we do agree on getting a nanny, I know there is no way I'd be able to sleep if I thought my baby was crying in a room too far away for me to hear.'

He'd thought of that too, in his time away.

He wanted Sophie to accept him for how he was. It worked both ways. He had to accept her for how she was too. He'd known from the start that she was different from everyone else who traversed his life.

She might not be the perfect wife he had wanted for himself but she would be the perfect mother for their child.

Sophie would protect and love their child in a way that would make it hardly aware of its father's remoteness.

'I need you to understand that if you won't have a nanny then you have to be prepared to do it all yourself,' he warned her. 'I'm not going to be one of those modern hands-on fathers. I am not designed that way and I work too-long hours.'

The light in her eyes dimmed a little more. 'Being hands-on would be good for you.'

'I doubt that and I doubt it would be good for the baby. I'll pay for any help you need but I won't be doing any of the work myself.'

Seeing she was prepared to argue, he cut her off. '*Carina*, we have months until the baby comes. I've had five very long days in the company of sharks and now I want nothing but to go for a swim and have some dinner.'

Her brows drew together. 'Did the trip not go well?'

Her obvious concern sliced through him. 'It was successful. The deal was signed.'

But the negotiations had been a lot tougher than he'd anticipated.

The Casillas brothers had always negotiated together. It had not felt right without Luis there, as if he were negotiating with an arm tied behind his back and a leg missing.

Luis had always been the counterpoint to him, charming the people who mattered, willing to play the game when Javier would rather cut his toes off than schmooze.

This time he'd had to play the role of good cop and bad cop in one.

He had managed it though.

His successful negotiations had been the proof he needed that he didn't need his brother in his life in any capacity.

'Will you have to spend a lot of time in South Africa when the development starts?'

'Yes. There will be occasions when I'm away for weeks at a time.'

He only just managed to cut himself off from suggesting that she accompany him on some of the trips.

The light in her eyes dimmed into nothing. Her lips drew tighter but then she hugged her arms around her chest and took a step back. 'I have something to show you.'

'What?'

'I have to show you, not tell you.'

He stared at her quizzically, then shrugged. 'Go on, then.'

He followed her down the stairs. As they walked, she kept up a light chatter about the nursery. 'I've also hired a local carpenter to make some bespoke furniture for it but he can't start working on it for a few weeks yet.'

'He had some scruples, did he?' he asked drily, wondering why she suddenly seemed so nervous.

She laughed but it sounded forced. 'I discovered that not everyone can be bought.'

You can't, he thought. In a world where money ruled he had married perhaps the only person on it who could not be paid for.

His thoughts turned to a blank when he stepped through the door Sophie opened that led into the smallest of his huge living rooms.

Lying on his solid oak floor, which he had treated twice a year to keep it in immaculate condition, fast asleep on a plastic oval bed heaped with blankets that dwarfed its tiny size, was a dog.

'What the hell is that?'

As he spoke, the dog opened its eyes and clambered to its feet.

'A puppy.'

He glared at her. 'I can see that. I meant what the hell is it doing in my house?'

'*Our* house.' The dog had padded to her feet and was scratching at her knee. She scooped it up and held it protectively in her arms. 'You said I should treat it as my home.'

'That does not give you licence to buy a dog.'

'I didn't buy it. I found it by—'

'You've brought a stray dog into my house?' he interrupted. 'What's wrong with you? Who knows what diseases it has?'

'*He* has no disease. I found him bleeding outside the gates of the house and took him to the vet. He was covered in puncture wounds, so we think he was mauled by another dog. The vet treated his wounds. Other than being terrified and in pain from the mauling, there's nothing wrong with him.'

'Why hasn't he been returned to his owner?'

'He isn't microchipped and no one's claimed him. It's likely he's been abandoned.'

He knew her intentions immediately. 'No.'

'Yes.'

'No. We are *not* having a dog.'

'We're not, *I* am. If the owner doesn't declare him or herself by the end of next week Frodo will be registered as mine.'

'Frodo?'

'He looks like a Frodo. He already answers to it.' Putting her nose down to the black rug in her arms' nose, she said, in word-perfect Spanish, 'You already know your name, don't you, Frodo?'

'Since when do you speak Spanish?' he asked in amazement.

'I've lived here for almost two years.'

'You've never spoken it before.'

'I made my wedding vows in Spanish. Besides, I haven't needed to with you,' she said, reverting back to her native language. 'Your English is much better than my Spanish. I speak Spanish with the staff.'

Realising he'd been distracted from the conversation at hand, he steered it back. 'He's not staying. We are not having a dog. You have enough to cope with.'

She could not argue with that logic.

Turned out she could.

'The baby's not due for five months. That's plenty of time to train it before the kumquat's born. He's only a puppy. The vet thinks he's about three months old.'

'What do you know about training a dog?'

'I grew up with dogs. And cats and guinea pigs and stick insects. I told you before you left for Cape Town that I always wanted to be a vet.'

Dios, the infuriating woman had an answer for everything.

But he would not be swayed.

'No. This is not a house for a dog. Think of the mess it

will create. I have antiques and artefacts worth millions.' In the corner of this room alone stood a statue of ancient Greek heritage. 'It can stay until next Friday to recover from its injuries. If the owner does not come forward it will go to a dog rescue and be adopted.'

His word final, he strolled out of the living room, intent on finding Julio and demanding to know why none of his staff had seen fit to warn him of his wife's doings.

'How can you be so *cruel*?'

He took a deep breath and turned back around.

His heart wrenched.

Sophie's eyes were bright with unshed tears, her chin wobbling. The puppy nuzzled into her hand. 'This is a poor, defenceless puppy who's been abandoned by its owner and now you want me to abandon it too. Well, I'm sorry but I can't. Look at the poor little thing. You think a stupid artefact is worth more than a *life*? If he doesn't stay then I don't stay.'

He stared at her with disbelief. 'I thought you didn't make threats.'

'I'm not making a threat. I'm telling you how it is. I will not abandon him. He needs me.'

'He does not need you. He needs a family, agreed, but it does not need to be this one.'

'It *does*!' She took a long inhalation, seeming to suck the tears back before they could fall. 'He's just settling in and now you want him to be uprooted all over again? What do you think that would do to him after everything he's been through? This house is *enormous*. We can compromise, we can put one of the living rooms aside for his use—this one would be perfect—and clear it of your precious artefacts so he can't damage anything, but if you won't compromise then I shall pack my things now because I am *not* giving him up.'

His incredulity grew. 'I don't understand you. I keep

thinking it isn't possible for you to have such a soft heart but then you threaten our marriage over a *dog*.'

She adjusted her hold on the ball of fluff. 'You don't understand me because you think my life has been nothing but unicorns and rainbows. You have no idea...'

'Are you telling me it hasn't been?' he demanded. 'You, with your talk of a house filled with animals, parents who love and support you... You have been raised with everything a child could desire.'

Everything he'd been denied as he'd been dragged around the world with a mother who'd barely tolerated him, never home long enough between tours for them to entertain a pet, a volatile father who'd idolised him but been so cruel to his twin.

Sophie could have no comprehension of his life and what he and his brother had lived through.

'Not everything, no,' she said tremulously, her face contorting. 'If you had read the documents I couriered to you for our wedding you would know I'm adopted. I was abandoned as a baby.'

His disbelief turned into shock.

He hadn't read the documents. He'd trusted they were in order and got his PA to send them to the officiant.

His brain began to burn as he suddenly wished he had read through them rather than tossing them to one side as if they meant nothing when what they had represented was the woman standing in front of him only just holding herself together over a dog.

He swallowed his lump-ridden throat. 'You were abandoned?'

She nodded, her throat moving as she stepped back to sit on the hand-stitched Italian leather sofa, cuddling the puppy on her lap.

If she hadn't just dropped her bombshell he would have

demanded she move the dog far away from his extremely expensive sofa.

'Don't think I'm playing for sympathy here,' she said. 'I would never play the victim card because I'm not a victim. I've been incredibly lucky and you're right, compared to yours, my childhood was unicorns and rainbows and I'm lucky that my parents—the people who adopted me—are all I can remember, but you said you don't understand me and maybe it's time you did.'

'How old were you?'

She drew her lips in and swallowed before answering. 'I was hours old when I was found. I'd been left outside a church in a village on the south coast of Devon. The vicar's wife found me—she'd come to lock the church for the night. I was lucky that she heard my cries because it was too dark for her to see me. I was put in the care of social services and fostered until my parents adopted me when I was eighteen months old.'

He swore, the burn in his brain at boiling point. 'How old were you when you learned this?'

Her hands stroked the dog's ears. 'I've always known. My parents never kept it a secret from me. My mum had cervical cancer in her early twenties and had to have a hysterectomy, so they couldn't have children of their own. They always said I was their miracle from God, delivered to them at His house.' She met his eyes and smiled. 'They're wrong—they're *my* miracle. When I think of all the couples out there that could have adopted me, I was given to a couple who loved me more than any child could possibly be loved.'

His legs becoming too shaky to support his weight, Javier staggered onto the armchair across from her. 'I'm sorry. I wish you had told me all this.'

'There's nothing to be sorry for. It's not something I talk about much because it's not something I remember.

My life as I know it began on the day of my adoption and it's been a wonderful life.'

Abandoned at her first breath and that was a wonderful life?

'Did they ever find your birth mother?'

'No. It was assumed she was a young teenager but she could have been anyone. No one came forward, no one was admitted to hospital with evident signs of recently giving birth, those who had given birth that day were all accounted for… She vanished. She could be anyone. My natural father could be anyone.'

'Do you wonder about them?'

'All the time.' Her smile saddened. 'I can't look at a new face without scanning it for a resemblance but I know I'll never find them. I pray my birth mother's alive and well.'

'You forgive her?'

'Whatever her reasons for giving me up, she must have been terrified and in so much pain.'

She meant it. He could see that clearly.

Sophie had forgiven the woman who abandoned her.

'How do you do it?' he asked starkly. 'How do you forgive? How can you open your heart so much when the people who should have loved and cared for you abandoned you as they did?'

'Because I was found.' She stared straight at him. 'I will never know the reasons and I accept that. But I was found and I was saved—my cries were heard. I've known that all my life and all my life I've sworn that I will never ignore any living soul's cries for help.' She pressed a kiss to the puppy's head, her eyes not leaving Javier's face. 'This little thing is as innocent and as helpless as I was and I will not abandon it.'

'No.' He sighed heavily.

Everything about Sophie made sense now.

He'd known she was different from the very start. He'd

seen that goodness and compassion shining out of her, the reverse lens of himself.

Where his heart had contracted into a shell, hers had expanded to embrace anyone who needed it.

But she was tough too. Her heart was as soft as a sweetened sponge but her spine was made of steel.

He did not doubt that she would take that abandoned dog and walk away from him if he refused to let it stay.

'No,' he repeated. 'I understand. The dog can stay. You can give it the love it needs.'

I can give you the love you need too, if only you would let me.

The thought popped into her head before Sophie could take it back but this time she did not push it away.

She rubbed the soft ears of the sweet, loving thing in her arms and wished she could hold Javier in the same way.

There was no point denying her feelings towards him any more. She loved him. She'd always loved him.

The heart was incapable of listening to reason and her heart had attached itself to Javier the first time she'd set eyes on him.

Whether he was capable of returning her love, she didn't know and told herself it didn't matter. His eyes had shone to see their child's nursery. He was developing feelings for their unborn child, she was sure of it. He'd agreed that Frodo could stay, so there was something akin to compassion inside him.

But Javier was far more damaged than the affectionate puppy in her arms.

Javier was reading the story he'd had emailed from a reporter who worked for an English newspaper when the landline on his office desk rang.

He pressed the button. He'd told his PA not to put any calls through unless it was his wife.

'I have Dante Moncada on line one,' she told him. 'He says it's important.'

He sighed. Dante Moncada was a Sicilian technology magnate who'd inherited a one-hundred-acre plot of land in a prime location off Florence that he had no use for and wanted to sell. Javier and Luis had been in talks about buying it from him. Nothing had been signed. It had been very early days in the talks when Javier and Luis had gone their separate ways.

Javier had held off doing anything about the deal while the lawyers set about severing the Casillas brothers' business, an issue that almost two months on was dragging interminably. Luis had communicated via their lawyers that he wanted to meet. Javier had refused. He never wanted to set eyes on his brother again.

His anger at Luis's treachery had not lessened in the slightest but he wanted a clean break for them.

He might despise the man he had loved and protected his entire life but he would not do anything to gain an advantage in the severance. The lawyers would ensure everything was split equally. That had been his firm belief until Dante had called him the week before to inform him that Luis had made a private offer for the land and asking if Javier would like to counter it.

His brother's latest display of treachery had speared him but he had hardened himself.

If his brother could be so disloyal as to hitch himself to the bitch who had worked to destroy him then Javier should not be surprised that Luis was going behind his back to steal business by targeting the clients they had cultivated together.

Two could play that game. And Javier would win.

'Yes,' he had informed the Sicilian. 'I would like to counter it. How much has he offered?'

Dante had given him the figure. Javier had increased it. He'd been waiting for a response ever since.

'Put him through,' he said now.

'Javier!' came the thickly accented voice.

'Dante. What can I do for you? Have you called to say you will accept my offer?'

'I'm coming to Madrid tomorrow for a few days of business. I've bought an apartment in your city, so I'm going to throw a party to celebrate. Come. We can discuss business then.'

His heart sank. Dante's parties were as legendary as his party-loving brother's.

He estimated this was Dante's tenth property purchase. The man would not be happy until he had property in every city in Europe.

'Will Luis be there?' he asked, stalling while he tried to think of an excuse.

Javier loathed parties. He despised watching people lose their inhibitions through alcohol, becoming worse versions of themselves. It was why he never drank. His father had been volatile enough without the alcohol he had come to depend on. He would never risk doing the same. He'd attended his brother's parties only so he could keep an eye on him and stop him doing stupid things, like swimming drunk.

He would not go to any function his brother attended.

'He's not answering my calls, so…'

The unspoken implication did not go over his head. If Luis was incommunicado then the land was Javier's for the taking.

'What's the address?'

Dante gave it to him, then finished by saying, 'Bring your wife. Everyone's dying to meet her.'

He would rather swim with sharks with a gashed knee pouring blood than take Sophie to that Lothario's party.

Giving a non-committal grunt, he ended the call and rubbed his temples.

He had a headache forming.

He put a call through to his PA for a coffee and painkillers, then turned his attention back to the computer screen.

Right then he had more important things to think about.

It had taken him weeks to find the information he'd sought. He could have passed the job on to one of his employees to oversee on his behalf but this was something he'd needed to find himself.

The reporter he'd paid to trawl through the archives of an English paper from Devon had finally come up trumps.

Before him was a copy of a report dated over twenty-four years ago, published before the Internet had been the go-to place for news reports.

Sophie's story had been front-page news. The news report gave all the details she'd skimmed over and omitted.

She'd omitted to mention, for example, that she'd been so severely dehydrated the doctors hadn't thought she would survive the night.

When she'd been found, she'd been swaddled in a pink blanket and left in an old box that had once contained crisps.

She hadn't been left on the church's steps where she would be easily found, she'd been left in the shrubbery.

It had been a miracle that she'd been found.

And she prayed for the woman who'd abandoned her and hoped she was alive and well?

Javier had no such compassion. He hoped, with every fibre of his being, that the woman who'd abandoned his wife to die had lived a short and painful life.

But there was no way of knowing. Sophie had been right that her birth mother would never be found.

That was something else he'd dug into these past few

weeks. The police investigation had been extremely thorough, he'd had to admit. They had left no stone unturned.

Everyone had been of the opinion that it had been a young teenage girl who'd been terrified to discover she was pregnant.

Why Javier had been so determined to delve into that period of Sophie's life when, by her own admittance, she had always accepted it as a fact of her life, he did not know, but it had been like a compulsion in him, a need to learn everything about her, to dig deep into her psyche and discover how someone who'd been left to die on her first day of life could contain such a beautiful, pure heart.

How could she live with him and his cold, vengeful heart without being repulsed?

How could she bear for him to even touch her?

CHAPTER TEN

'WHAT ARE YOU READING?'

Sophie, sitting cross-legged on the bed with a pillow and laptop on her lap, looked up and smiled to see Javier in the doorway. She'd been so engrossed she hadn't heard him get back from work.

'I'm looking at veterinary nurse courses for after the baby's born,' she said, turning the laptop around to show him. 'I'm trying to work out if it's feasible.'

He strolled over to perch next to her. 'To train as a vet nurse?'

She nodded. The days she spent with Frodo had reignited her love of animals and her old dream of working with them.

His brow furrowed. 'Why would you do that?'

'I thought you were supportive of me working. All that talk about nannies—'

'I didn't mean it like that,' he cut in. 'I meant why would you want to be a vet *nurse*?'

'Do you think it would be too much?' she asked anxiously. 'From what I've read, I'll be able to do most of the studying from home—'

'No,' he interrupted again with rising exasperation. 'Why train to be a vet *nurse* when you've always wanted to be a *vet*?'

'It takes years to train to be a vet. Besides, I haven't got the qualifications.'

'Then get them.'

She blinked a number of times. The educational options that had been available at her ballet school had not included those that gave an entry into veterinary school. She would have to go back to basics. 'Just like that?'

'Why not?'

'Javier, it will take me years to get the necessary qualifications *if* I can get them…'

'Why would you not get them? You're not stupid. If you can be a professional ballerina when your heart wasn't in it then there is no reason whatsoever that you can't achieve the qualifications needed to train as a vet.'

'But then I'll have to spend years studying at university. I have to think of our child and—'

'Stop making excuses,' he snapped. He pulled the laptop off her and deleted the link she'd been reading before closing the lid. 'You've always wanted to be a vet, so stop making excuses and for once in your life start putting yourself first. If it takes ten years for you to do it then so what? It took Luis and me almost that long to start earning serious money from Casillas Ventures but we never entertained the idea of giving up and you shouldn't either. This is your dream, *carina*, so grab it.'

She stared at him, her heart blooming at his logic and defence of her dreams.

'Wouldn't it bother you?' she asked eventually.

'Should it matter if it did?' he countered.

'You're my husband. Of course your opinion and feelings matter.'

'More than your own? Is that not what you did before? Put your dreams to one side because you thought more of your parents' feelings than your own?'

'It wasn't exactly like that,' she murmured, embarrassed.

He raised a disbelieving brow.

'Okay, maybe it was a little,' she conceded. 'They loved watching me dance. It meant so much to them, so what else could I have done? They gave me so much. They gave me a home and a family. They gave me love.'

'Did you think if you went against their wishes they would withdraw that love?' he asked with an astuteness that stunned her.

Javier displayed such indifference to her that it was a shock to realise he actually paid attention to everything she said. And everything she didn't.

She sighed and pulled at her hair. 'I don't know. I remember worrying about that when I was little and fully comprehended what being adopted meant. They chose to bring me into their lives, so there was always that dread that they could then choose to give me back.' She'd forgotten that long-ago irrational fear, an unintended consequence of her parents' complete honesty about her beginnings. 'I think…it was this pregnancy that showed me their love for me was truly unconditional.'

'How?'

She shrugged ruefully. 'I was afraid to tell them. They're very spiritual. They believe greatly in marriage coming before children and I was afraid they would think less of me.'

'Did you think they would reject you?'

'Not on a rational level but it was there in the back of my mind, yes. I hadn't even realised how scared I was to tell them until they practically squashed me with their hugs.'

'Are they the reason you were a virgin when we conceived our baby?'

It was the first time this had been acknowledged out loud between them.

Sophie met his steady gaze and gave a tiny nod.

He extended a hand as if to reach for her belly, then

changed his mind before he could touch it and got to his feet. He rolled his neck. 'It is time you thought of your own needs rather than always thinking of others. Our child will be much happier for having a fulfilled mother than one who settled for second best. If you want to be a vet then be a vet. Better to try and fail than never have the guts to try in the—' He cut himself off, now looking at the floor-length navy-blue dress hanging on the dressing-room door. 'Have you been shopping?'

Disconcerted by the sudden change of subject, she took a moment to remember.

'I popped out this afternoon. I meant to put it away but got distracted with all the vet nurse stuff.'

She moved the pillow off her lap and scrambled off the bed to get the dress.

Frodo, who had taken to following her like a shadow and been dozing by the bed, woke and jumped up in an attempt to grab hold of it but she whipped it out of his way and took it into the dressing room.

Javier followed her and rested his hand on the doorway.

She waited for him to make a comment on the puppy being in their bedroom, which he had effectively banned and she had effectively ignored if he wasn't in, but instead he asked, 'What's the dress for?'

'The party.'

'What party?'

'Dante Moncado's party tomorrow night.'

He was silent for a beat before asking, 'How do you know about that?'

'The invitation was hand-delivered this morning. It was addressed to both of us, so I opened it. I've put it on your dressing table.'

He took hold of it and read it silently. Then he put it back down and rubbed his face. 'We've been invited for business purposes. You won't enjoy it, *carina*.'

'How do you know that?'

'You're pregnant.'

'Yes, pregnant. Not dead.'

'It will be full of rich, posturing idiots. I'll go on my own, conduct our business and come back.'

Her heart thumped, the warm fuzzy feelings generated by Javier's brusque insistence that she should follow her dreams squashed back to nothing. 'Do you know, you haven't taken me anywhere since we married. Are you ashamed of me?'

'What a ridiculous thing to say. And I have taken you out.' He'd taken her to a business dinner where partners had been invited.

'A business dinner doesn't count. You haven't taken me out—out socially.'

'This is a party I've been invited to for the sole purpose of business, not for social reasons.'

'But it's an actual party. It says so on the invite. And my name's on the invite too. I want to go.'

'I didn't realise you were a party person,' he said stiffly.

'You never asked and we haven't been invited to any…' She narrowed her eyes, suspicions rising. 'Unless you didn't tell me about them.'

He stared back.

It took such a long time for him to answer that her suspicions became a certainty.

He had turned invitations down without mentioning anything about them to her.

'I never go to parties,' he eventually said in the same stiff voice. 'I don't drink. Who wants to watch people get drunk and make fools of themselves?'

'I do.' She hated that her voice sounded so forlorn and made an effort to strengthen it. 'If you won't take me then I really will think you're ashamed of me.'

Would he have these qualms about taking Freya with him? Sophie wondered.

He'd probably only said all that stuff about her becoming a vet so she would be occupied and out of his hair for the next ten years, she thought bitterly.

It hadn't crossed her mind that he wouldn't want to go to the party. She was well aware that her husband was not one of life's great socialisers but had assumed he would be willing to attend a party being hosted only twenty minutes from their home. Since his return from Cape Town he'd taken to giving her prior warning of meetings and functions he had planned that would take place outside normal office hours. It was a gesture that had given her hope. Slowly their marriage had been starting to feel like a real one. His attitude now put her right back to square one.

He had nothing booked in for tomorrow night.

All she could think was that he didn't want to show his second-choice wife to his peers.

So proud had he been of having Freya tied to him that he'd thrown a huge party to celebrate their engagement.

He hadn't invited a single guest to their wedding. They hadn't had a single guest to their home since they'd married.

'I am *not* ashamed of you.' He groped at his hair.

'Then prove it and take me,' she challenged. 'We don't have to stay for long. You can conduct your business and I can meet some new people and then we can come back.'

Even Frodo, sitting at her feet, looked at Javier expectantly.

Javier noticed. 'What about the dog? We can't take him to a party or give him free rein alone in the house, and you won't put him in a crate.'

Sensing victory, Sophie smiled and opened the bedroom

door. Marsela, the youngest of the household staff and a live-in one to boot, had been cleaning the spare bedrooms a short while earlier. She called for her.

A moment later, Marsela appeared.

Frodo spotted her and bounded over, his tail wagging happily.

'Have you got any plans tomorrow night?' Sophie asked.

'No. I have a date with a box set.'

'Any chance you could dog-sit Frodo while you watch it?'

Marsela's eyes lit up. 'I would love to.'

'Thank you!' Turning back to Javier, Sophie fixed him with a stare. 'So, are we going?'

His face like thunder, he gave a sharp nod, turned on his heel and stormed from the room.

She let him go, her heart battering manically against her ribs.

She could take no joy in her victory, however widely she pasted her smile.

Forcing his hand into taking her made it a hollow one.

Javier stepped out of the door his driver held open for him, then extended a hand to Sophie.

She took hold of it with a smile of thanks and, careful of her dress, climbed out.

Then she straightened, carefully smoothed her hair, which she'd styled into loose curls, and said, 'I think this is the part where we go in.'

He breathed deeply and gave a nod. 'Prepare yourself. Everyone will be watching you.'

'I'll be fine,' she said with a brittleness to her tone he'd never heard before.

He would learn soon enough if she was right.

She certainly looked the part.

When she'd appeared from the dressing room, it had

taken everything he had to stop his mouth gaping open like a simpleton.

The light had shone behind her, making her glow like an angel.

Her floor-length dress, navy-blue mesh lace, low cut at the top to skim her ever-growing cleavage and puffing out at the hips, fitted her as well as if it had been made bespoke for her.

A more perfect vision of glowing beauty he had never seen.

The thought of lecherous eyes soaking in her beauty for their own delectation had made him feel like a thousand bugs were crawling over his skin.

He'd wanted to pull that dress off and make love to her so thoroughly that his scent would be marked in her, a warning to all others to not even look let alone touch.

It had been a fearsome thought that had him clenching his hands into fists and walking out of the bedroom before he could act on it.

They had not exchanged a solitary word on the drive over.

Resting a hand lightly to her back, he led her through the old, exclusive apartment building, where a concierge escorted them to the elevator that would take them to Dante's new penthouse.

The huge, open-plan space the party was being hosted in was already filled with guests.

The buzz of chatter increased in volume and excitement as Javier guided Sophie through the throng, his eyes seeking Dante, already keen to get this over with and get the hell out.

They could stare and gossip about him as much as they liked but his wife was not a piece of meat to be studied and gaped at.

He'd turned down four parties on their behalf since

they'd married. Never minding his loathing of large gatherings, he'd had no intention of putting Sophie in the firing line of the inquisitive eyes he was always subjected to at these things. Now all he could do was get through his business as quickly as he could and get her out of there.

Swiping them a glass of fruit juice each from a passing waiter, Javier was taking his first sip when Dante approached, the easy smile so reminiscent of Luis's smile on his face.

'I knew you'd come,' he said smugly, before introducing himself to Sophie and putting his hands on her bare shoulders to kiss her cheeks in turn.

Javier clenched his jaw and forced himself to breathe, turning his mind away from the impulse to punch Dante in the face.

Get a grip of yourself. He's only greeting her the way he greets everyone; the way all polite society people greet each other.

His fingers still itched to punch him though.

Dante called his date over. She was a statuesque model, famed as the elite designers' clothes horse of choice.

Her eyes fixed on Javier with a gleam he recognised, part fear, part curiosity, part desire.

He only just managed to stop his face twisting with disgust.

The woman was beautiful, that could not be denied, but she did not hold a candle to Sophie. No one did. No one could.

Dante turned to the woman. 'Lola, look after Sophie while I steal her husband away. We have business to discuss.'

If Sophie was bothered about being palmed off, she didn't show it. She smiled at Javier and gave an almost imperceptible wink.

'I'm afraid I have disappointing news,' Dante said

as he led him into his private office. 'The sale's off—temporarily.'

'Oh?'

Dante opened a cabinet and pulled out a bottle of Scotch and two glasses. 'An illegitimate heir has come out of the woodwork. Her lawyers say she has a claim to the inheritance and therefore a claim to the land.'

'And does she?'

Dante's eyes glittered menacingly. 'I will make sure she doesn't.'

Javier shrugged. He couldn't care less about Dante's problems. All he cared about was taking his wife home.

'Drink?'

Javier raised his palm and shook his head.

'Oh, yes, I forgot you don't drink. That was always Luis's forte. And speaking of Luis, I'm surprised you're not in the Caribbean with him. Or are the rumours that you two have ended more than your business relationship true?'

Javier did not dignify that with a response.

His private business was no one else's concern. Dante might be comfortable sharing personal confidences; that did not mean Javier had to follow suit.

'When do you anticipate solving the problem with the illegitimate heir?' he asked, putting the conversation back on the business footing it should have stayed on.

'A few weeks. Maybe a month. I'll call you when it's done. I should warn you though, Luis has asked that I give him the opportunity to make another counter-offer.'

'Whatever he offers, I will top it,' Javier said flatly.

Dante raised his glass and grinned. 'I do love a bidding war.' He knocked back the Scotch, grimaced and poured himself another. 'My money would be on you winning.'

Despite himself, Javier's curiosity got the better of him. 'Why?'

Luis might be the more easy-going of the Casillas brothers but when it came to business he was as razor sharp as Javier. It was what had made them such a good team.

'When I saw him the other week he was all loved-up.' His grimace that time had nothing to do with the drink. 'His heart's not with the business, it's with his new wife...'

'He's not married yet,' Javier interjected.

Dante's surprise appeared genuine. 'You don't know? Luis and Chloe married yesterday. They released a statement about it this morning.'

Sophie stared around at the crowd of beautifully dressed people all so comfortable in their wealth and standing in society and felt as she'd done on her wedding day: like an imposter.

She had been so looking forward to this party, had been determined to ignore Javier's grumpiness about it and embrace something new in this new life of hers, something they could share together.

Lola, the cat-eyed supermodel, had abandoned her after a few minutes of not-in-the-slightest-bit-subtle questioning that Sophie had stonewalled with non-committal answers all delivered with a smile so as not to hurt her feelings.

But, honestly, did Lola really expect her to share confidences about her husband with a complete stranger?

She wished she could have a glass of the free-flowing champagne but she hadn't touched a drop of alcohol in her pregnancy and was not about to start now.

Sliding her phone out of her clutch bag, she messaged Marsela to check on Frodo, pretending not to see the inquisitive stares still being directed at her from all corners.

She missed her little shadow. He was such a playful comfort to her during the days when she felt Javier's absence like a hole in her heart. She didn't have a clue what breed he was, some kind of small poodle cross. The vet had suggested a DNA test on him but she'd decided not to. Whatever Frodo was, he was hers and she loved him. He responded to her love in a way she wished so badly that Javier would.

Javier hadn't even bothered to comment on her appearance. She'd made such an effort for him, desperately wanting him to be proud to have her on his arm, but he'd looked her up and down and left the room.

A slap on the face would have been kinder.

'You look lost.'

The man who'd approached her, who could only be described as a silver fox, smiled.

She smiled back at the friendly face that matched the unmistakable English voice. 'Not lost. Just soaking up the atmosphere.'

'Javier abandoned you, has he?' he said, his words and tone implying he and Javier were acquaintances.

They wouldn't be friends. Javier did not have friends.

'He's talking with Dante.'

'Were you not invited to join them?'

She pulled a face. 'It's about business, something I know nothing about.'

'Ah, yes, you're a ballerina. I remember watching you perform in *The Sleeping Beauty*.'

'Did you?' she asked dubiously. She had been a part of the *corps de ballet* and utterly inconspicuous in her costume.

He suddenly looked sheepish. 'My wife—she's Spanish—dragged me along to it. I only know you were in it because she told me on the drive over here. Dante told everyone that Javier would be bringing his new wife. You're the star attraction, you know.'

'Am I?'

'But of course. He's been hiding you away for months. We all wanted to see you for ourselves and make sure that it wasn't a vicious rumour that he'd snared another young English ballerina as his bride—' He cut himself off and winced. 'My apologies. That was callous of me.'

'No, it's fine.' She adopted nonchalance. There was no point in making a fuss over what everyone was thinking. Javier's engagement to Freya had been announced with huge fanfare. His marriage to Sophie had not even had an official press release. 'I'm the second-choice young English ballerina bride.'

'Maybe second choice but I would hazard a guess that you're not second best.' His eyes dipped to her belly. 'Because I can see the other rumour is true too…unless this is where you tell me you're not pregnant but had an extra helping of cheesecake.'

Sophie burst into laughter. 'Yes, I'm pregnant and the great thing about it is I can have as much cheesecake as I like.'

'You won't find any at this party if Dante's girlfriend organised the catering.' He guffawed. 'Let's see if we can find some food that isn't just fit for rabbits. We might find my wife somewhere too. I think she's abandoned me.'

Glad of the friendly company, Sophie was about to follow him when she spotted Dante in a corner, chatting with a group of people.

If his meeting with Javier was done with…

She craned her neck, then craned some more.

Where was Javier?

Javier steamed down the dark streets, his hands rammed in his trouser pockets, dodging the evening revellers spilling onto the pavements from the bars and clubs.

His blood raced with rage. Pure, undiluted, unfiltered rage.

He had finished his meeting with Dante with his brain burning to learn Luis had married.

The faint hope he'd unknowingly held onto that his brother would come to his senses and end things with Chloe had been stamped out.

He had married her.

Prepared to grab Sophie and insist they leave immediately, he had been confronted with her talking to a handsome man he vaguely recognised.

Not just talking to him either, he thought grimly, remembering the laughter that had shone on her face.

She'd been enjoying the man's company so much that she'd been oblivious to her husband standing only ten feet away watching them.

In that moment he'd had a choice.

Either he could go to them, lift the man flirting so shamelessly with his wife into the air and hurl him out of a window or he could leave.

He'd left without looking back.

His phone vibrated in his pocket, the third time it had rung.

He pulled it out and, not looking at it, turned it off.

Right then he did not want to see or speak to anyone.

He did not trust himself.

Right then the urge to inflict the pain coursing through his veins on someone else was too strong to risk, that much self-awareness he did have.

He walked for miles, detouring through pavements he hadn't trod on since he was a teenager and his and Luis's only means of transport had been their legs.

Thirteen years old they'd been when Madrid had suddenly become their home. To escape the grandparents who'd been little more than strangers to them, they had explored the new streets they lived on, a tight unit, protecting each other as they had always done.

In every corner lay a memory.

Eventually he could put it off no longer.

He slowed his pace as he walked the long driveway to his home and climbed the marble steps.

Before he could open the door, it swung open.

Standing there, her face white with fury, was Sophie.

CHAPTER ELEVEN

Sophie didn't know whether to throw her arms around Javier in her relief or push him down the steps.

She'd searched everywhere in that huge apartment for him, refusing to believe he would have left without her.

She'd only confronted the truth when she'd gone outside to look and Michael, his driver, who'd been waiting for them, had gently told her Javier had chosen to walk home.

That had been three hours ago.

The realisation that he'd abandoned her with a roomful of strangers had knocked all the wind out of her.

She'd been too shocked to be angry.

Then the time had passed while she'd waited for him to come home and the anger had built.

That anger had been giving way to concern when she had spotted him in the CCTV camera feed she'd sat herself in front of.

Now she didn't know how she felt, just that she was so full of contrary emotions that she would either cry or scream.

He stared back at her, his features taut, a pulse throbbing on his jaw, hands rammed in his pockets, breathing heavily.

He was the one to break the oppressive silence.

'You need to step out of my way.'

She shook her head. 'No.'

'Sophie, at this moment I do not trust myself to be anywhere near you. Get out of my way.'

Holding her ground, she folded her arms across her chest. 'No.'

He swore loudly.

'I'm not moving until you tell me why you left me at the party without a—'

'You didn't look as if you'd care,' he spat back, suddenly springing to life to brush past her and enter the house.

She pushed the door shut and turned in time to see him storm up the stairs.

Barefooted, holding the skirt of her dress up, she pursued him.

She might be pregnant but she was still quick and she reached the bedroom door before he could slam it shut and lock her out.

'Sophie, you need to leave,' he told her tightly as he held the door frame, his knuckles white, refusing her admittance. 'Sleep in another room tonight. We will talk in the morning when I am not so angry.'

'When *you're* not so angry? I'm the only one who should be angry. You abandoned me.'

He winced at her choice of word.

Good. So he damned well should wince.

'I told Michael I was walking home. I knew he would get you back safely.'

'You *left* me there. You humiliated me in front of all those people who were already laughing at me.'

'If you felt humiliated you did a fine job of hiding it. You looked like you were having a damned good time without me. Now, I need you to go.'

'I am not going anywhere. You're not shutting me out, Javier. Why did you leave? Tell me!'

'It was either leave or throw your boyfriend out of the window. Would you have preferred I do that?'

'What are you talking about?'

'I saw you, *carina*. With that man. Laughing with him.'

She suddenly remembered the Englishman she'd briefly chatted with, the only bright spot of her entire night. 'My God, were you jealous? Is that what this is all about?'

'Right now, I do not know anything other than that I cannot trust myself to be in the same room as you and you need to get the hell out of my sight until I am calm.'

Struggling for air, her heart thumping, Sophie took a step back, saw Javier loosen his hold on the frame of the door and, before he could close it, used the advantage of surprise to push past him and into the bedroom.

'Get out!' he howled.

'No, I will not! You're behaving like an idiot. All I was doing was talking. Or is that illegal now? Do I need your permission to talk to a man? Or maybe you would like to cover me in a bin bag when I leave the house? And what do you even care?' she continued, her voice getting louder as she gathered momentum, all her bottled-up feelings rising like poison inside her. 'I'm just a possession to you, aren't I? The second-best wife, not as good as your first choice, not as *perfect*, not good enough to be taken out in public with pride because I'm only a second-rate ballerina, not as pretty—'

'That's enough!'

His roar echoed through the walls as he lunged for her, taking hold of her biceps and leaning down to her, his breath hot on her face. 'Don't you ever put yourself down again, do you hear me? You are worth a million Freyas. Don't you see that? You are the most incredible, special person I have ever met in my life and it scares the *hell* out of me that one day I might hurt you. I felt *nothing* for Freya and she felt nothing for me and that was safe. You do not make me feel safe. You make me feel things I should never feel and the thought of anyone hurting a hair on your beautiful head makes me want to rip heads off bodies and that's what I've been fighting against since you walked into my life because I know the biggest danger to you is *me*.'

If a heart could burst then hers just did.

'Oh, Javier,' she whispered, a tear spilling down her cheek as she put a trembling hand to his face and gazed helplessly at the eyes that swirled with more emotion than she could have ever hoped to see in them. 'You are not your father.'

Javier stared at the beautiful, open face that haunted his every waking and sleeping moment and suddenly he was lost.

Pushing her against the wall, he kissed her with every ounce of feeling contained inside him.

Her lips parted to welcome him and then they were clinging together, her arms tight around his neck as he fed on her kisses like a condemned man taking his one last meal.

A desperation he had never felt before overcame him, a need to touch and be touched, and it hit him like a fever in his brain, the blood that had sprung to life all that time ago for this beautiful, incredible woman awake and crashing through his body, refusing to be denied or ignored any longer.

He lifted her into his arms and cradled her in them, gazing into her eyes as he carried her to the bed, marvelling with wonder at the colours and emotions he saw in their depths.

How had he never seen them before?

And she stared back with equal intensity.

Laying her on the bed, he put his palm to her cheek and caressed the satin skin his fingers always yearned to touch.

And then he kissed her again.

And then he was drowning.

Working as one as they devoured each other with their mouths, they stripped their clothes off, throwing them without a care for where they landed, the need to be naked in each other's arms too strong to care for anything but this moment, this here, this now.

Because whatever fever had him in its grip, it was in Sophie too, there in the hunger of her kisses and the urgency of her touch.

He wanted to feel every part of her, to give this woman who sang to his heart all the passion and love that had broken free from its casing for her.

He opened his ears to her sighs and let them seep into his senses and then he opened *all* his senses to her.

He was helpless to do anything else.

And she opened her senses to him.

Her fingers traced lightly over his chest, exploring him, her mouth following, her nose brushing over his skin to breathe him in, touching him in a way he had never been touched before.

Every breath of her mouth to his flesh seeped deep inside him to the bones that lay beneath.

He brushed his lips over every part of her too. He inhaled the scent of her skin so deeply that it became a part of him. He kissed her breasts and felt their weight in his hands. He ran his fingers over her belly, a distant part of him awed at what lay inside it but only a distant part because this moment was not about their child, this moment was for her, for him, for them.

When he inhaled the musky heat between her legs, he almost lost himself entirely.

How had he blocked it out so well before and for so long?

It was a scent he would remember for the rest of his life.

If he could love any woman it would be this one, he

thought dimly, pressing a kiss to her hip before pushing himself back up to stare into the pale blue eyes once more.

Sophie gazed into the eyes staring at her with such hunger and felt every part of her expand and contract.

She pressed a hand to his face. He rubbed his cheek against it and kissed her palm. And then he kissed her mouth with such possessiveness that her heart bloomed.

Every part of her bloomed.

Her skin was alive from the flames of his touch, everything heated, scorched, her veins lava…and that was lava reflecting back at her in the depth of his stare and she realised that for the first time she was staring right into the heart of this man she loved so much.

The sense of detachment that had always been there… gone.

This was Javier as she had dreamed, touching her and making love to her as if she were the most revered thing in his life, holding her so close their skin could become one and their hearts unite.

His eyes stayed open, boring into her when he entered and…

Oh, the *sensation* that erupted within her…

This was everything. *Everything*.

Javier had no recall of entering her; found himself buried deep inside Sophie with her arms locked around him and his hands resting against her cheeks.

The expression reflecting back at him as he made love to her, the wonder, the tenderness…

The void he'd fought against for so long welcomed him into its depths.

He submitted to it.

Javier woke with a start, opening his eyes to the darkness.

Sophie was draped over him, the delicious weight of her thigh hooked over his, her arm locked around his waist.

His heart pounded, his guts felt as if he'd been punched and for a moment it was as if he'd forgotten how to breathe.

What the hell had he done?

He'd lost all control of himself.

With Sophie.

He pinched the bridge of his nose and fought to inhale.

His movement must have disturbed her for she shifted, pressing herself closer to him; as if it was even possible for her to get any closer.

She could. She did.

He didn't know if she was fully awake when her lips brushed against his neck and she rolled on top of him, her cheek pressed to his, her silky hair falling softly onto his face, or if she was in the midst of a dream.

It felt as if *he* were in a dream of his own when she sank onto his hardness, a dream that had him holding her tightly, possessively, while deep in the back of his mind came the thought that if anything happened to this woman he would want to die.

Sophie stretched a leg out and smiled before she'd even opened her eyes.

This was the start of a new day that would mark the beginning of her new life.

This was the day that marked the true start of her marriage.

The breakthrough she had so longed for had finally been reached. Javier had opened himself up to her and then he had made love to her. Truly made love to her, with his heart and his mind as well as his body.

She still wasn't foolish enough to believe it would be plain sailing from here on in, but what they had found together under these sheets and the connection that embraced them tightly together…

She opened her eyes and her heart sank as if it had a weight attached to it to find the empty space between them.

Javier had moved to the edge of the bed, his back to her.

It wasn't his mesmerising face she was greeted with after the best night of her life but his cold shoulder.

She blew a puff of air out and told herself to put a curb on her imagination.

He'd rolled over? He'd probably been uncomfortable. He probably hadn't even done it consciously.

But that was a huge distance. To reach him she would have to stretch a hand out...

Before she had the chance to do so, he suddenly pushed the sheets off and climbed out of bed.

He strolled to the bathroom and shut the door without looking at her.

Disturbed but telling herself she was being silly, trying her hardest not to make a big deal out of something she didn't even know what, Sophie hurried to the dressing room and threw on an oversized T-shirt and a pair of leggings.

She needed to act normal.

Before she could leave the bedroom, he appeared from the bathroom, a towel around his waist.

'Good morning,' she said brightly.

She was answered with a grunt.

'I'm going to check on Frodo. Do you want a coffee?'

'I'll get one when I come down.'

'Okay... Is everything all right?'

He cast her a quick glance. 'Why wouldn't it be?'

She shrugged, not knowing how to answer, and backed out of the room.

Frodo was asleep at the bottom of the stairs. He woke up at her footsteps and wagged his tail excitedly to see her.

At least someone was happy to see her, she thought unhappily, scooping him up.

Javier was being…well, he was being exactly how he always was first thing in the morning: moody and distant.

He wasn't a morning person.

She'd try to add an extra sugar to his coffee to sweeten him up, she decided, brushing away the anxiety now gnawing in her belly.

She found Marsela laying out the breakfast stuff in the dining room and thanked her for looking after Frodo. 'I'll sort some money out for you when I go back up to get changed,' she promised.

Marsela looked positively affronted. 'I don't want your money. It was my pleasure to look after him.'

On impulse, Sophie planted a kiss to the sweet Spanish woman's cheek, the exact moment Javier came into the dining room.

Marsela hurried out.

He took a seat at the table and swiped at his phone. 'You are too familiar with the staff,' he said, not looking at her.

'Am I?'

'Yes.'

She sat opposite him and put Frodo down at her feet. 'Marsela's my age. I like her. If I want to be friends with her then I shall.'

His jaw clenched but he said nothing further.

Breakfast was brought in and placed between them.

'I was thinking of taking Frodo for a walk in the park later. Do you want to come?'

'I'm going to the office.'

She tried to cover her disappointment. 'On a Saturday?'

'I have much to organise before my trip to Cape Town.'

'That's not for another week,' she pointed out.

'I'm looking to bring it forward.'

'Any reason?'

'To get things moving quicker.'

'We've got the scan on Wednesday,' she reminded him.

He hadn't promised he would be there, only promised that he would try. She had wanted to push it but had held back.

If this had been a conversation held an hour ago she would have pushed it, secure in the cocoon of passion they had created together.

'If I can come then I will come,' he answered shortly.

She was bewildered at the change in him.

The cold, emotionless man was back with a vengeance.

He drank his coffee and got to his feet.

'You're going to the office now?'

'Yes. I'll let you know if I'm not going to make it back for dinner.'

Stunned and hurt at the indifference being displayed, she watched him walk out before suddenly calling out to him. 'Javier.'

'What?'

She almost recoiled to see the coldness in his eyes.

'Last night…' But she couldn't say anything more. Her throat had closed up.

'What about it?'

She shook her head. 'Nothing.'

He left without saying goodbye.

Sophie was grateful to have Frodo as a distraction. Although still small, he was unrecognisable as the damaged puppy she had found on the kerb. Playful and loving, he had a marvellous time playing in the park with the other dogs and Sophie soon found other owners to talk with. For the first time, a complete stranger asked her if she was pregnant.

The thickening around her waist was turning into a small but recognisable swell, more pronounced on her petite frame than it would otherwise be. She was barely halfway through the pregnancy. There was still a long way to go.

But she had experienced flutterings in recent weeks, real, unmistakable signs that the baby inside her was growing strongly, that it was a *baby* in there.

On the short walk back to the house, she bought a newspaper from a vendor she passed. Javier would laugh at her for absorbing the news the old-fashioned way but she much preferred to read it in paper format than through a screen.

Reading the paper would be another good distraction. She no longer had to avoid the news, the Javier-Freya-Benjamin saga relegated to history.

Except it wasn't.

Her insides twisted with pain for her husband.

Page nine contained a half-page story on the marriage of Luis Casillas and Chloe Guillem.

CHAPTER TWELVE

Javier arrived back late. It was too much to expect Sophie to be asleep but still he hoped.

He worked out for an hour in his gym to increase his chances and showered in the adjoining wet room.

The hurt he'd seen in her eyes had cut him in two.

Last night had been a terrible mistake and it was down to him to put their marriage on the footing it had originally been, for Sophie's sake even if she had trouble understanding it.

One day she would thank him for it.

It was with no surprise that he found her sitting on the bed, not even pretending to read or be doing anything that indicated she hadn't been waiting up for him.

She was still dressed.

He should be relieved. He'd half expected to find her dressed in lingerie, intent on seducing him.

Thuds of dread battered in him.

'How was your walk?' he asked, needing to cut through the strange, tense atmosphere he'd walked into.

'Fun.' She gave a half-smile. 'How was your day?'

'Long.'

'You're tired?'

'Exhausted.' Yet still wired. Electricity charged through the room but the buzz he felt on his skin was different from the usual charge he felt when with her and which he always tried valiantly to ignore.

'Javier… Have you seen the newspaper reports?'

'About Luis getting married?'

She nodded. 'You have seen them, then.'

'Dante mentioned it last night.'

There was sympathy in her narrowed stare he did not want to see.

'Why didn't you tell me?'

'Why would I have done?'

He hated the flash of hurt that rang back in her eyes.

'Because I'm your wife.'

'It isn't important.'

'What isn't? Luis getting married or that I'm your wife?'

His jaw clenched in the way that told Sophie he wouldn't answer.

He really was shutting her out.

'Did you rearrange your trip to Cape Town?'

He jerked a nod.

'And?'

'I leave on Tuesday.'

The swirl of nausea in her stomach was so powerful Sophie almost vomited from it.

She swallowed a number of times before saying, 'You're not coming to the scan, then?'

'No.'

Breathing deeply, she put her head in her hands before looking back at him. 'Was that deliberate?'

His jaw clenched again.

'We made love last night,' she whispered.

The pulse on his jaw throbbed.

'We *did*,' she stated in a stronger voice, in case he was inclined to deny it.

She would not have him deny it.

'We made love and it was wonderful. You said things

to me I never thought I would hear. I thought we'd turned a corner. Was I wrong? Because today you have treated me like I mean nothing to you and I need to know if it's a case of you pushing me away because you're struggling with your feelings for me and have been trying to process them or if it's because you have *no* feelings for me.'

His breaths had become heavy. 'My feelings for you are…complicated.'

That wasn't a denial of feelings, she thought, experiencing a tiny surge of encouragement. 'How?'

'Last night… I could have hurt you.'

'But you didn't. You made love to me.'

He grabbed the back of his neck, the lips that had kissed her with such tenderness and passion pulling together. 'There is something inside me that's dangerous.'

'You said that last night.'

'And it's true. It has always been in me. I spend my life fighting it.'

'Has it beaten you before?'

His eyes found hers. 'Yes.'

'Who?'

'Some boys. When I was fourteen. They followed me and Luis home from school and made some comment about our mother. It was a bad day as it would have been our mother's birthday. I beat the crap out of them. One of them was hospitalised with a concussion.'

'Anyone else?'

'No.' His eyes gleamed with malice. 'I have wanted to though.'

'But you haven't.'

'Only because I keep tight control over it. I keep emotion out of my life. Last night should never have happened. My emotions got the better of me. It will not happen again.'

'Emotions aren't dangerous.'

'They are for me.' The malice vanished. 'Every time I

look in a mirror I see the truth. I am my father's son and my father was ruled by emotions.'

'But you are not your father. You look a little like him…'

'I am his double.'

She shrugged. 'Not that I can see. But even if you are, you can't help who or what you look like. I haven't got the faintest idea who I look like or whose blood runs in my veins.'

'Then you have no legacy to live up to or break free from.'

'I have nothing to hide behind.'

His hooded stare narrowed. 'What do you mean by that?'

She swallowed again before summoning her courage to say, 'I think you're using your father as an excuse to keep me at a distance.'

The rage that flashed in his eyes almost made her wish she'd kept her mouth shut.

'My father killed my mother,' Javier snarled.

Dios, how could she think that? As if he would ever use the bastard who had given him life as an excuse for *anything*.

'He put his hands around her throat and strangled her until she had no breath left in her. I spent my childhood trying to protect Luis from the worst of himself because my father despised him and needed no excuse to beat him—he threatened to throw him into a pool and let him drown once and he damned well meant it. My father loved only one person—me, but only because I looked so much like him. The genetic pool favoured me to him. He would rub my hair and tell me I was just like him.'

Every time his father had done that Javier had cringed inside but also, to his eternal shame, thrilled in it.

He'd thrilled at being loved by the man who'd caused such terror to his brother.

He'd hated his father with every fibre of his being.

But he had loved him too.

What had scared him the most was that his father's assertions were right. That Javier *was* just like him, on the inside as well as on the surface.

'He recognised something in me and my mother saw it too,' he continued. 'I *know* she did and if you looked closely enough you would see it too.'

He drew long breaths in as he stared at the woman he would give his last breath to protect.

She blinked rapidly, her chin wobbling, throat moving. 'I have looked closely,' she whispered. 'I don't see it.'

'Then you are a blind fool and I will not endanger you or our child by allowing what occurred between us last night to happen again.'

'Meaning that you intend to keep me at a distance?'

'Meaning our marriage will continue as we first set out.'

She rubbed her eyes with both hands and took a deep breath before fixing pain-filled eyes on him. 'I was afraid you would say that. I've spent the day thinking about what it would mean and trying to work out if it's something I can live with and I'm sorry but I can't. Not any more. I've tried. I think you have too. But it's not enough.'

'What are you saying?'

'That we need to admit defeat and call it a day.'

He reared back. 'You want to leave me?'

'No.' Her throat moved again. 'I don't want to but I know I have to. I don't care what you say, I don't believe for a minute that you would ever hurt me, but if you don't believe that and you keep holding me at a distance I think there is a very real chance you will destroy me.'

He didn't understand. She could be speaking in tongues for all he comprehended.

She must have read what he was thinking on his face for she laughed as tears suddenly rained like a waterfall down her face. 'And you say *I'm* the blind fool? I *love* you, Javier. I love you so much that it's killing me inside.'

'How can you love me?' he asked, disbelieving...not *wanting* to believe. 'I've treated you like dirt.'

'Not all the time.' She pushed the tears away with the palms of her hands. 'I always understood your actions were deliberate. I'm not a fool, whatever you believe. But you listen. You compromise when you can. You've been supportive...so supportive. I cannot tell you how much that has meant to me, the way you tried to convince me not to give up dance when the baby's born, then when you understood my dream was to be a vet and your belief and encouragement that I could do it... You said I need to put myself first and you're right, I do. Me and the baby.'

She rubbed her face one last time and climbed off the bed.

Somehow, despite her tears, there was a dignity about her.

'I can't keep putting my dreams on hold for other people. My wonderful parents who rescued me, Freya... I regret none of it but now I know things have to change. *I* have to change. I refuse to put my whole life and heart on hold for you. I deserve better than to spend my life pining for you to fall in love with me when you won't give your feelings a chance. Our child deserves better too. I thought that given time you would at least fall in love with our baby but I don't see how that can happen when you won't allow it and that breaks my heart. I understand if you can't love me, but to deliberately withhold your love from our child...?'

As she spoke, the tears stopped falling and she grew in stature. But anger was coming through too, a whole gauntlet of emotions showing on her.

'That's cruel and it's weak. Too scared to love a helpless baby?'

'I am not scared,' he disputed, furious at the accusation and her twisting of things. 'I am trying to protect you both!'

'Oh, yes, you are.' The tears had gone completely now, her face as hard as he had ever seen it. 'You are scared to love, Javier Casillas. It's not me or the baby you're protecting, it's yourself, and not because you're too damaged but because you're too scared to let us in.'

She practically danced into the dressing room, reappearing moments later with a large suitcase in her hands.

'You planned this?' His anger had risen so hard inside him he could choke on it. 'You already knew you were going to leave?'

'No. I hadn't planned to leave but I knew there was a good possibility of it.'

'Where are you going to go?' he demanded to know. 'It's the middle of the night!'

'I'll check into a hotel.'

'It's the middle of the night,' he repeated through gritted teeth.

She put the case down and opened the door. 'And why's that? That will be because you spent the entire day avoiding me. You should be grateful—with me gone, you won't have to hide from your own home any more. You can have a lovely time roaming your lovely *empty* house, which perfectly matches your empty life.'

'I was not—'

'Will you cut the crap?' she suddenly screamed, hair whipping around her shoulders as she turned wild eyes on him. 'As soon as anyone gets close to you, you push them away. You're already pushing our baby away and it's not even born! You brought your trip to Cape Town forward to avoid going to the scan with me and seeing your own child for yourself! If you won't let it into your heart and give it the love it deserves then it's better if you stay on the periphery of our lives and let me love it for the both of us.'

'You had better not be threatening to take my baby from me,' he warned. 'You will not deny me access to it.'

'Says the man who wanted to shove it in the east wing far away from us so you wouldn't be disturbed by its cries?'

'We signed a contract!' If Sophie wanted to leave then good riddance but she would not take his child from him.

'I don't care! Our baby is *not* a possession, it's a living being who needs love and security, not a father too scared to let anyone into his heart, who screws over his best friend and cuts his own brother out of his life rather than admit to his mistakes and admit that he needs them. Because, guess what? You need your brother.'

'Do not bring Luis into this,' he roared. 'He's the disloyal one who walked away from everything we built together, not me.'

'Do you think he threw away your relationship and business on a whim?' she asked scathingly, throwing her hands in the air. 'At least he's not scared to open his heart, and he's lived through everything you have. He *loves* Chloe and if you had any concept of what real love is you would understand that and stop condemning him and accusing him of disloyalty. The world is not against you, Javier, whatever you think, and if the day comes when you see that too and are willing to open your heart to be a real father to our child and understand that you are not, I repeat *not*, your father, come and find me and you can have all the access you want.'

Extending the handhold for the case to wheel it beside her, she left the room without a backwards glance.

'Get back here,' he hollered down the corridor, loud enough to wake the live-in staff in their self-contained flats in the basement. 'We are not done yet.'

'Oh, yes, we are.' Sophie would not look back. She didn't dare.

Already the outburst that had exploded out of her from nowhere was fading and she could feel her legs weakening as her resolve faltered.

She must not let it falter.

'If you leave you will never come back. The next time you see me will be in a courtroom.'

She did not answer.

Her throat no longer worked.

Frodo was at the bottom of the stairs, sitting up and looking at her. For once his tail didn't wag to see her.

From upstairs a door slammed.

She squeezed her eyes shut, took the longest breath of her life, then messaged for a cab.

In the living room that had been cleared of all Javier's precious artefacts, she gathered Frodo's stuff together, put his lead on him and took him outside and down the long driveway.

The electric gate opened when she reached the bottom.

The cab pulled up.

Holding her dog tightly on her lap, she took one last look at the house she had hoped so hard would be her home.

And then the tears flowed freely.

The meeting was not going well. The government official Javier had brought in to look over the blueprint of the development plans before it was officially submitted was being deliberately obtuse and obstructive.

The lead architect, a rising star in Daniele Pellegrini's architectural empire, was looking everywhere but at Javier, clearly afraid to meet his eyes.

And so he should be scared. This was his fault and Javier would make damned sure Daniele knew it.

Aside from himself, five people sat in this meeting

room. Incompetent fools, the lot of them. If they couldn't produce the blueprints to an earlier deadline without cutting corners they should never have agreed to do so.

His phone buzzed.

He snatched it off the table without looking at it, instead glaring at the people around the table. 'I shall take this call and when I get back I expect to be given solutions, not additional problems. Understood?'

He strode from the meeting room without waiting for an answer.

A few minutes alone-time would do him good. Hopefully it would purge his need to bang heads together.

He'd wanted to bang a lot of heads these past few days. His punching bag had had almost forty-eight hours of continual pounding.

He should have brought it to Cape Town with him.

His phone had stopped buzzing. He swiped it and saw his accountant's name flash up.

He was about to call him back when his phone buzzed again, this time a message alert.

This time, the name that flashed on his screen was not his accountant but his wife.

Heat rushed to his head.

Javier had not seen or heard from Sophie in four days.

He was damned if he would open it. From now on, all contact between them would be done through their lawyers.

As soon as he got back to Madrid, he would call his lawyer and get the ball rolling, couldn't think why he hadn't already done so.

That damned black mist had blinded him.

Damn her, they had signed a contract agreeing joint custody in the event that they split up, something *she* had insisted on. And now she wanted to break it. Not him, *her*, the woman who had professed her love for him in one breath, then thrown unfounded accusations at him with the next.

Clearly her declaration of love had been a lie, although for what purpose he could not begin to imagine.

He had been honest with her from the start. He had bent over backwards to find compromise and protect her and their child.

Sophie was not taking their child from him. He would never be a hands-on father but he would be a father and he would not allow her to deny him that.

In his mind, he would be a father who would share an evening meal and impart authority and wisdom. He would be a father to look up to.

He would not allow himself to get close enough to be a father who was feared.

About to shove his phone in his pocket, he instead found himself swiping the message.

There was no text. Only a video attachment.

Rubbing violently at his scalp, he stared at the screen in his hand, then, again working of its own volition, his thumb pressed to open it.

He blinked hard, not quite recognising what he was seeing, his heart hammering in his throat, wonder increasing as the golden frames rotating in front of him suddenly became clear.

Little hands were curled in balls at the sides of a round head where eyes, nose and a mouth were clearly delineated, the lips slightly parted as if his tiny baby was snoring gently in its cocoon. A short neck, then a round belly moving up and down, tiny wiggling feet that ended with ten long toes…

Something hot stabbed the backs of his eyes and he blinked a number of times, inhaling deeply, fighting for air.

In his mind flashed the acute pain that had shone in

Sophie's eyes when she had realised he'd deliberately arranged things so he would miss the scan.

Had she sent this as a rebuke?

A taunt?

He pinched the bridge of his nose and pulled shuddering breaths into his lungs.

He felt winded.

Sophie did not do taunts.

He dragged more air into his lungs.

It was only a scan. Only an image.

He needed to pull himself together.

He had a meeting to finish.

Five pale faces sat in silence on his return.

He took his seat and rubbed his hair.

All the anger he'd carried with him since Sophie had left had gone.

Now there was nothing but an acute pain clenching in his guts.

He'd taken his anger out on these people, he realised with a stab of guilt.

He'd been behaving in the exact manner he despised.

Instilling healthy fear was one thing—as a rule he didn't need to do anything but raise an eyebrow to achieve that—but acting like a pig-headed toddler having a tantrum was quite another.

'I owe you all an apology,' he said heavily. 'I realise I pushed for the plans to be completed early and that you have all worked your backsides off to achieve this.'

He lifted the landline phone and pressed the button that put him through to his PA, who had accompanied him on the trip. 'Can you arrange for refreshments to be brought in for us from Giglis?' Giglis was a deli a few streets away. 'Ask for enough to feed a dozen people, and make sure to buy some for yourself.'

Turning back to the startled faces before him, he got

back to his feet. 'Food will be with you shortly. Eat, then take the rest of the day off. Get back together tomorrow to find solutions to the problems when heads are clear. When everything is ironed out, let me know and we can video conference. I'm going home.'

He didn't need to be there.

Sophie had called him out correctly that he avoided his home when she was there.

She was gone now. He didn't need to avoid it any more.

'What are you doing?' Javier asked when he walked into his dressing room and found Marsela rifling through the clothes Sophie had left behind.

She spun around to face him, the colour draining from her face.

He guessed she hadn't received the message he would be returning early.

She stammered an apology, which turned into a garble. Eventually he was able to gather that Sophie had asked her to pack the possessions she hadn't had the time to take with her and forward them to England.

He held his palms up and backed out of the room. 'Carry on. Use our usual courier for it.'

This was good. Excellent in fact. His room, his home, were all becoming his own again. No more opening his bathroom cabinet to find ladies' toiletries in there, no more walking down his stairs avoiding tripping over a dog, no more clock-watching in the office knowing Sophie was at home waiting for him to return.

The nursery door was open.

He'd blanked it from his mind since Sophie had left but as he passed it something inside caught his eye.

A large white wardrobe, dresser and crib had been delivered in his absence, all placed against a wall ready to be set in their new places.

Swallowing a huge lump that had formed in his throat, Javier was about to call for Marsela to explain where the items had come from when he suddenly remembered Sophie telling him she'd employed a local carpenter to craft the baby's furniture by hand.

That had been right before she had introduced him to Frodo.

Right before she had told him about her beginnings and he'd feared his heart would splinter.

On the wall beside the tall wardrobe rested a full-length mirror with an edging crafted in the same design as the other bespoke items of furniture.

He dragged his feet to it and stared at his reflection.

From as far back as he could remember everyone had always said how much like his father he was and how much like their mother Luis was. That resemblance had always been something Javier had hated. After their father had killed their mother, he had actively avoided mirrors. Who wanted to see the face of a murderer? Such was his loathing that when he did come across one he would squint his eyes to turn his appearance into a blur.

Sophie didn't see the face he saw or that others saw.

He narrowed his eyes and peered closer.

What did she see?

How was she able to penetrate the surface to find a part of himself even he didn't know was there?

He thought hard, remembering the day she had first come to him with the legal documents that would have tied him to Freya. He remembered the soft compassion that had rung out at him when he'd looked into her eyes.

No one had ever looked at him like that.

No one had ever looked at him the way Sophie did.

She looked for the good in everyone.

She'd ignored all the stories about him, ignored his

warnings and all the evidence of his cruel nature and given her heart to him.

Why?

How could she trust her feelings the way she did and trust that the light would break through when all he ever saw was darkness?

But he had seen light with Sophie. Moments of joy when his guard had dropped enough to allow the light to filter through the dark.

How could she put her heart and life in the hands of a man with the potential for such violence…?

His heart made a sudden thump.

The night of Dante's party…

The green-eyed monster had reared its head straight after his discovery that Luis had married. He'd been so full of angry emotion but he hadn't lashed out. Even at that awful, low point he hadn't raised a hand to her; he'd swallowed all that angry passion and made love to her instead, real love, not a mechanical act of going through the motions.

He hadn't raised a hand to the man he'd thought was flirting with her either, and why had that been? Not just because even in his rage he'd known on a fundamental level that to strike out would be wrong, but because he'd known Sophie would be horrified and that his actions would hurt her.

Sophie could not bear to see another's pain. It would have hurt her as much as his father's beatings of his twin had hurt him.

And he could not bear to see her pain.

He would never lay a finger on her, just as he'd been unable to lay a finger on Luis when they had had that terrible row.

Javier was not his father.

He could never hurt someone he loved.

CHAPTER THIRTEEN

NIGHT SETTLED IN MADRID.

Javier sat on the floor of the nursery his wife had created for their unborn child, unable to move. His reflection shone back at him, lit by the light of the growing moon that cast shadows that loomed ominously over him.

Time became nothing.

The weight that had compressed in him on his wedding day had become a leaden pit that crushed all his organs.

Thoughts and memories he'd never allowed freedom to roam in his head had rebelled and now crowded in on him.

The ache in his guts was far beyond mere nausea.

And still he didn't move.

Not until the sun made its first peak on the horizon to start its ascent and clear the darkness did he break out of his stupor.

Sophie was *his* sun.

Without her, his life would remain cold and barren.

Without her, he would never feel the warmth she shone on his skin.

Without her, he was nothing.

He needed to go to her.

But first, there were things he needed to do. Wrongs he needed to right.

He needed to cleanse his conscience.

Breathing heavily, he groped for his phone.

He dialled from memory the number he had deleted from his contacts months ago.

The sleepy voice answered after three rings. 'Javier?'

His throat had become so tight it was an effort to speak. 'Hello, Luis.'

Javier took a deep breath, then rang the bell of the sea-fronted villa along the Mediterranean coast, less than thirty kilometres from Spain's border with France.

He was expected. The bell still echoed when the door was opened and a member of the household staff admitted him into the spacious, modern home.

Footsteps sounded in the distance, hurried, nearing towards him.

Then the gangly form of Chloe Guillem...no, Chloe Casillas appeared.

'You're early,' she said stiffly, making no pretence at pleasantries.

He did not blame her.

'I apologise,' Javier replied carefully. 'The drive was quicker than I anticipated.'

She scowled but then her face softened as Luis appeared from a side door.

The look on her face was all Javier needed to know that she loved his brother.

And now he too looked at his twin, struck by the changes he saw before him.

His perennial tan had deepened, his hair lightened by the sun...

But these were only surface changes.

His brother radiated happiness...but also wariness and curiosity.

There was none of the malice Javier had expected to see and which he knew he deserved.

'I'm going to leave you two to it,' Chloe said, planting

a kiss on Luis's lips, then adding a whisper Javier knew he was meant to hear. 'Call me when he's gone.'

'Not my biggest fan?' Javier asked wryly when it was just him and his brother alone for the first time in months.

Luis ran a hand through his hair and pulled a face.

'I don't suppose I can blame her,' Javier said heavily.

Luis stared at him for a long time, eyes narrowed. Then he gave a sharp nod, the beginnings of a smile hovering on his lips. 'Let's get the pleasantries over with, shall we? Then we can talk.'

After a quick tour of the house Luis and Chloe had moved into only days earlier, both having developed a love of beach life from their time in the Caribbean, they moved outside to sit on the wall that overlooked Luis's private beach. Stilted small talk had been the extent of their conversation up to this point, catching up with each other's lives, both learning for the first time that they were going to be uncles as well as fathers.

'When do I get to meet Sophie?' Luis asked. 'I know I must have done when she danced for us but, to be honest, I don't remember her.'

Javier swallowed. 'I don't know. She's in England. She's…left me.'

'Oh.'

'It's my fault. All my fault. Everything is my fault.'

Luis's silence gave voice to his thoughts on that.

'Did you speak to Benjamin?' Javier asked, breaking it.

He had tried calling him a number of times but his messages had gone unanswered. In the end he had called Luis again and asked if he would speak on his behalf and arrange a meeting for them.

Luis nodded. 'He is expecting you this evening.'

'Thank you.'

More silence fell, broken only by the waves crashing onto the shore.

'Why did you do it?' Luis asked quietly.

He'd been waiting for this. 'Rip Benjamin off?'

'Yes. Was it deliberate? Did you deliberately fail to warn him of the change in terms?'

They both knew the answer but Javier knew his brother needed to hear it from him.

And he needed to say it too. 'Yes.'

Luis nodded thoughtfully, his gaze fixed out on the sea. 'And did you know the night we signed the contract with Benjamin that he thought he'd signed it under the original terms?'

Javier closed his eyes.

'Yes,' he admitted heavily. 'He mentioned the percentage before I left. I knew then that he hadn't read it. I didn't see fit to warn him or correct his mistake or give him the chance to renegotiate because I was a stone-cold bastard who didn't care that he was suffering over his mother. I had no empathy. I was…dead inside.'

He'd been dead for so long that he hadn't noticed Sophie bringing him back to life until it was too late.

'The only person I cared about was you and I harboured a resentment towards Benjamin for the closeness you had. A part of me had always resented him. I see that now.'

It was an admission that left his veins cold.

'You were jealous?'

'I resented that you could have fun with him.'

'You were too busy trying to keep me out of trouble for fun.' Luis's own voice had the same heaviness to it. 'I regret letting you bear that weight.'

They both exhaled at the same time. Luis gave a grunt-like laugh, then said, 'What do you feel now?'

'Sick with myself. I shut down after our mother died. I was afraid I was like our father and that if I let emotion in I would become him. Instead I became a monster in a different form.'

Another long silence fell between them.

Javier knew Luis was thinking the same as he, of their childhood, two boys who'd shared a womb before being born into a world where the only option had been to survive by sticking together and protecting each other.

Eventually Luis said, 'Our parents screwed with our heads long before our father did what he did. But it doesn't have to define us.'

Javier thought of Sophie, again, the woman who had no idea who her real parents were, where she came from or why she'd been abandoned. She had never allowed that beginning to define her or close her heart off.

'Does Chloe make you happy?' he asked.

'More than I ever dreamed possible.'

'Good. You deserve happiness.'

Luis looked at him. 'So do you.'

He shrugged. 'I think it might be too late for me. I pushed her too far this time. I think she has let go.'

In his heart he knew she would never keep their child from him. But as for their marriage…

That he did not know how to fix.

'Talk to her. She might surprise you.'

'Sophie has never done anything but surprise me.'

Much later, Luis showed him to the door, promises made to get together very soon and work out a plan for their future.

'Good luck with Benjamin,' his brother said as he embraced him.

'Thank you. And thank you for getting him to agree to see me.'

'No problem. I'm just grateful to have you back in my life. I've missed you.'

'Did you approach Dante with the offer for the land deliberately?' Javier suddenly remembered to ask.

Luis gave his first genuine smile, the cheeky grin

Javier had grown up looking at. 'I had to flush you out somehow.'

'How high would you have gone?'

'As high as was needed for you to come to your senses and talk to me. I never would have guessed a woman would have done that for me.'

He managed a returning smile. 'Neither would I.'

Sophie concentrated hard on the document she was reading at her parents' kitchen table, wishing she'd asked for the English version rather than the Spanish. She wouldn't have to keep looking words up for their meanings. But it was necessary doing it like this.

Once the baby was born she would return to Spain. It was going to be her home. If she wanted to be a vet there she would have to become fluent in all aspects of the language.

There was a rap on the front door.

Getting to her feet with a sigh, she closed the living-room door and went to answer it.

The top half of the front door was frosted glass. Through it she could see her visitor was a person of immense height and width…

Her heart thumped, then set off at a canter.

Keeping a tight grip on the door handle, she tried to breathe.

You're being ridiculous. It isn't him. It couldn't be him.

Javier had sent her only one message since she'd left him and that had consisted of two words—Thank you—after she'd emailed the scan.

It had taken him two days to write those two words.

She had read those two words so many times her eyes had blurred.

From that, nothing. No call, no message. Every letter dropped through the post in the eight days she'd been in

England and every ping of an email had brought a thud of dread in her, fear that this would be the moment she received a legal notice of his intention to fight for custody.

It had taken every effort to keep her resolve and ignore the plaintive voice in her head pleading with her to apologise.

She mustn't.

Their marriage was over. All she could do was pray Javier came to his senses and realised he had it in him to be a real father to their child. Freya's phone call three nights ago had given her cause to hope. Now she had to hope this unexpected visit was the start of that journey and not the first blood of a nasty legal battle.

She counted to five, fixed a smile to her face and opened the door.

The smile would not sustain itself.

The moment she stared into the light brown eyes she'd missed more than she had thought possible everything swelled inside her and it took every ounce of effort not to burst into tears.

The features she had soaked into her memory bank were taut, his jaw clenched in that, oh, so familiar way.

She couldn't tear her gaze from his eyes. She had never seen that expression in them before. Such…softness…

'Hello, *carina*,' he said in a tone she'd never heard before either. It contained the same softness as his eyes. 'I apologise for turning up unannounced. May I come in?'

It seemed to take for ever before she could get her throat to work. 'Yes, of course.'

Her legs as she led him inside felt drugged. Her head felt drugged too, as if a thick fog had been injected into it.

So dazed was she at Javier's unexpected appearance that she'd forgotten Frodo was in the living room until she opened the door and he went bouncing round the room, his tail wagging as he then ran circles around Javier.

He gave a grunt-like laugh and picked the puppy up, Frodo immediately licking his cheek with frantic excitement.

'He's grown,' Javier said, carrying Frodo to a seat at the dining table and sitting him on his lap. Then he stared at Sophie, his eyes drifting down to her ripening belly. 'And so have you.'

Stunned at the welcome Frodo had given the man who had rarely paid him any attention, equally stunned at the fuss the man in question was making of him, Sophie could only nod vaguely. Her bump seemed to have exploded these past few days.

'Can I get you a drink?'

'No. Thank you.' He grimaced. 'Please, sit down. We need to talk.'

She took the seat next to him but backed it away to create distance and bunched her hands together on her lap, desperate to contain the tremors in them.

'How have you been?' he asked.

Miserable. Scared. Heartsick. 'I'm good. Baby's good. She's learned how to kick.'

'You can feel it?'

She nodded. 'She's very active, especially at night. I think she's asleep now though.'

'She?' His eyes widened. 'We are having a girl?'

'I didn't ask but the scan was so clear it was obvious. The nurse confirmed it for me.'

His features tightened. 'I'm sorry I wasn't there.'

'So am I.' She felt no malice towards him, only a deep sadness.

Her anger had barely lasted longer than the walk down the driveway from his home, its residue long put to bed.

'Freya tells me you've seen Benjamin.' That was what her old friend had called to tell her; their first real conversation since Freya had left Javier for Benjamin. Or, as

Sophie now knew, since Freya had been *kidnapped* by Benjamin.

Kidnapped or not, Freya had been delirious with happiness. She had also been astounded at the contrition Javier had shown when he had turned up at their chateau.

Hearing his name had been a stab to Sophie's heart.

The next stab had come from Freya's demand to know what magic she had woven to make the ice-cold Javier Casillas admit to his faults and ask, in all sincerity, for forgiveness.

It was hearing this that had given Sophie the kernel of hope about Javier and their child.

But she had refused to let that hope gain traction.

The pain at the recognition that Javier would never change, would never love her, would always push her and the baby away…that pain had lanced her like no pain she had ever felt before. She could not put herself through that again.

He blew out a long puff of air and put Frodo on the floor.

Then he straightened in his seat and looked at her. 'I needed to apologise to him. I behaved… I can make all the excuses in the world but it doesn't change the fact that I did rip him off and for that there is no excuse. It was me. No one else.'

'How did he take your apology?'

'He refused to take the money back from me but he had the grace to listen. I hope one day he can forgive me.'

'I hope that too,' she said softly. 'I'm glad you accept what you did and that you had the guts to apologise. It couldn't have been easy for you. What made you do it?'

'Apologise?'

She nodded.

'You did.' He rubbed a hand through his hair. 'You've done something to me.'

'What?'

'You've…infected me. The way you see the world. What you lived through, your abandonment. That could have made you bitter and cold like me but you turned it into a force for good. You refuse to see the bad; you turn it over and see the sunny side.

'You and I… I've been doing a lot of thinking…' He rubbed his hair again. 'I have treated you very badly. I cannot tell you how sick I am with myself. I thought my behaviour was justified because I was trying to protect you but I see the truth now and the truth is that you were right—the only person I was protecting was myself.'

He closed his eyes. 'I shut myself off from emotions so long ago it is hard for me to be any other way. I do not know how to love. I've never been taught how to love a person in the way they should be loved. I want to try but…' His throat moved and now he fixed desolate eyes on her. 'I need your help. I want to love our child…that scan you sent to me, it made my heart hurt. It hasn't stopped hurting since. I know what I need to do but I don't know how. Please, *carina*, help me.'

Stunned, her own heart aching with pain at this admission she knew must have cost him everything to make, Sophie squeezed her balled hands even tighter to stop them from touching him.

'Of course I will help you,' she whispered.

How could she not? This was what she had demanded from him when she had walked out of his home: when he was ready to be a father to come and find her.

He was ready.

He had come and found her.

Whatever her feelings for this man, he was her daughter's father and she would do whatever it took for them to forge a close and loving relationship.

He blew out a heavy breath. 'In the back of my mind, I keep thinking, what if I'm like my parents?'

Now she did reach for him, unballing her hand to rest it on his arm. 'You are not your father.'

His eyes narrowed with intensity. 'I know. You have shown me that. I do not fear hurting our child any more but I do fear...'

'Fear what?' she asked gently, moving her hand down his arm to wrap her fingers around his.

He squeezed. 'My mother never liked me. She never abused me the way my father abused Luis but she was never warm to me. My parents each had their favourite and we both suffered in different ways for it. What if I don't like our child?'

'You will. You will like her and you will love her.'

'How can you be so sure?' he asked, his expression haunted.

'That pain you feel in your heart? That's your heart opening itself up for you to love her. Your love for her is already in you. When she's born and you develop a bond with her, that love will grow, I promise. And I will help you. She'll have to live full-time with me in the early months as I'm hoping to feed her myself, but that won't stop you being with her. You can see her as much as you like and stay with us for as long as you like. My door will always be open to you.'

Javier stared into the only eyes in the world that had ever looked at him and seen the man he could be and not the steel façade he'd built to protect himself.

'Will you not come home to me, *carina*?'

Her silence before answering went on so long that the beats of his heart turned into the chimes of doom.

'I can't,' she whispered. 'I'll return to Madrid once the baby's born and I'll live there with her like we planned but I can't live in your home again.'

His throat closed so tightly he had to swallow numerous times before he could say, 'I thought you wanted us to be a real family.'

'I did.' Gently removing her hand from his, she put it back on her lap. She stared down at it, no longer looking at him. 'I'm happy that you want to be a real father. I swear on everything I love that I will help you however I can to love our daughter and be the best father you can be but I can't move back in with you.'

'You said you love me.'

'That's why I can't move back in.'

He stared in disbelief at the bowed head but it wasn't until he saw a tear drop onto her lap that it suddenly became clear to him.

Shifting forward, he gently took her cheeks in his hands and raised her face to look at him. 'Do you still love me?'

Her lips and chin wobbled as more tears sprang out of eyes that had turned red. She jerked the smallest of nods.

Her voice was so low he had to strain everything to hear her. 'I have loved you for so long that I can't remember when I didn't but it isn't enough, not when you can't love me back. I can't put myself through that again. It would destroy me.'

'I am the biggest fool in the world,' he murmured, bringing his nose to rest against hers, his heart pounding as hard as it had ever pounded. 'I let you walk out of my life when you are the best thing to have ever happened to me. The single best thing. You told me once that your parents regard you as their miracle from God. You are *my* miracle, *carina*. You are an angel sent to save me from myself and I love you so much that it isn't just my heart that hurts, it is all of me. I ache from missing you. I pushed you away so many times that I wouldn't blame you if you didn't believe me but, *mi amor*, I have loved you from that first time I looked in your eyes. You have brought light into the darkness of my life—you *are* my light. I am sorry beyond words for the pain I have caused you and I swear, on everything I love, that if you give me—*us*—another chance

I will be a better man. I will be the husband and lover you deserve. I swear it. I love you, Sophie, with my whole life.'

Her tears had soaked his hands, drenched them with the misery and pain he had caused.

He would give his life to take that pain from her.

'How can you be so sure?' she whispered.

'Because I feel it.' Finally, he allowed himself to smile. 'A wise woman once told me that sometimes feelings are all we can trust.'

An arm suddenly hooked around his neck. She pressed her forehead to his and stared so deeply into his eyes that he felt the beam from it touch his soul.

And from that look, his soul flew up to his mouth and spilled out everything contained in it. 'I want to make love to you, to touch you, to taste you, to sleep with you locked in my arms every night for the rest of my life. You look at me and I feel I could walk on water. I want to fight the wolves that would harm you and I would give my life to keep you safe.

'Trust me with your heart, *mi amor*,' he begged. 'Trust it to me and I will keep it safe for the rest of my life.'

Her eyes continued to bore into him, searching, searching, searching until he was stripped of everything but the essence of who he was...

And then she smiled.

It was a smile of such pure, radiating joy that the last of the darkness that had lived in him his whole life was pushed out for ever.

When her lips found his and crushed him with her kisses he hauled her tightly into his arms, this angel sent to save his soul and warm his heart.

'I love you, Javier,' she whispered as she trailed kisses over his face. 'I love you more than I thought it was possible to love someone. I want to spend the rest of my life locked in your arms. I want to fight the wolves that would do you harm. I want to kiss you until all the pain in your heart has gone.'

'You have already done that, *mi amor*.'

Just having her in his arms like this and hearing her sweet words of love made his heart feel reborn.

And, as her lips found his and the passion between them reignited, Javier's last conscious thought before he carried her upstairs and made love to her was that this was the start of their new life.

With Sophie he had found his heart and his soul.

Four months later...

The midwife took his daughter from his beautiful, tired wife's chest and held her out to him.

Javier stared at the tiny form with the surprisingly long, kicking legs and allowed her to be placed in his arms.

Terrified of dropping her, it took him long moments before he dared to breathe.

He soaked in every millimetre of the delicate face, the creases, the rosebud lips that had parted in a wail when she had entered this world minutes before, stared with awe at the soft bundle of dark hair on the crown of her head, marvelled at the sharp little nails on the little fingers that had a tight grasp of his thumb...

His heart expanded. It bloomed...

And he fell madly in love.

EPILOGUE

'I CAN SEE IT!' called Sophie's daughter, Fiona, a sturdy six-year-old who was sporting an outstanding front gap in her mouth, her top two front teeth having both fallen out on the same day and absolutely *not* with any help from Fiona. None at all.

Fiona was pointing at the nearing island, her little feet tapping with excitement.

'I see too!' her brother squealed.

'No, you can't,' scoffed Christopher, Freya and Benjamin's son, rightly pointing out that three-year-old Roberto was lying his head off as there was no way he could see over the railing to Marietta Island.

The three families were heading for their annual summer break on Luis and Chloe's Caribbean island, a tradition amongst them since Luis had insisted they all go five years ago, to thrash out the past once and for all and put it to bed for good.

There had been no thrashing out. Whether it had been the magic of the sun or whether it had been because Benjamin had come to understand Javier's contrition was genuine—a donation of the exact amount Javier had ripped him off by had been made to a charity of Benjamin's choice in Benjamin's name; two hundred and twenty-five million euros, plus interest—but before Sophie had known what was happening she'd witnessed her gruff husband slapping Benjamin on the back, the two men laughing uproariously.

She still wasn't quite sure if she'd imagined that. She loved her husband dearly but he still wasn't one for seeing the funny side of life. He was getting better though. Three children were teaching him that.

And there he was, emerging from the sun lounge, baby Raul in his arms.

Her heart lifted to see him as it always did and as she knew it always would.

Seven years of marriage and she had never once regretted her decision to give him that second chance.

It hadn't been easy but then she had never thought it would be. The damage done to her husband had been too deep and too ingrained to be erased overnight. She had learned when to give him space and as the years had passed he'd needed less and less of it. In return, he had been nothing but supportive over her studies. She'd got the qualifications needed to study as a vet but by then she'd had Fiona and was expecting Roberto, had added to their menagerie of animals with two more dogs and come to the conclusion that it was caring for the animals themselves that she loved to do and so, with Javier's support and backing, had opened an animal rescue centre instead. She employed Marsela to manage it for her.

She grinned at him.

He grinned back and held Raul out to her. 'One clean baby.'

She grinned again. 'See, I told you we didn't need to bring the nanny along.'

He grunted but there was a sparkle in his eye. 'You never said I would be taking on her chores.'

'I can see Thomas!' Fiona suddenly bellowed, now waving her arms frantically at her cousin, Luis and Chloe's eldest son born only weeks after her—which, naturally, meant Fiona was always in charge when the cousins were together—who was waving back with equal intensity. Running up behind Thomas were the four-year-old twins Gregory and Georgina, lagging behind their brother because they were punching each other every few steps.

The yacht's captain brought the vessel to anchor next to Luis's, which matched theirs for size—something incredibly important to both men, she and Chloe liked to snigger about—and then Freya appeared clutching her belly and looking a little green with morning sickness, Benjamin, who had no interest in yachts, preferring his growing collection of classic cars, supporting her, and they all followed the excited children onto the golden sand.

That night, wrapped in Javier's arms on a beach chair, watching her children and their cousins wading under the moonlight, Sophie sighed with contentment.

Sometimes it felt as if her heart could explode with happiness.

* * * * *

MILLS & BOON

Coming next month

THE ITALIAN'S CHRISTMAS HOUSEKEEPER
Sharon Kendrick

'The only thing which will stop me, is you,' he continued, his voice a deep silken purr. 'So stop me, Molly. Turn away and walk out right now and do us both a favour, because something tells me this is a bad idea.'

He was giving her the opportunity to leave but Molly knew she wasn't going to take it – because when did things like this ever happen to people like her? She wasn't like most women her age. She'd never had sex. Never come even close, despite her few forays onto a dating website which had all ended in disaster. Yet now a man she barely knew was proposing seduction and suddenly she was up for it, and she didn't care if it was *bad*. Hadn't she spent her whole life trying to be good? And where had it got her?

Her heart was crashing against her rib-cage as she stared up into his rugged features and greedily drank them in. 'I don't care if it's a bad idea,' she whispered. 'Maybe I want it as much as you do.'

Continue reading
THE ITALIAN'S CHRISTMAS HOUSEKEEPER
Sharon Kendrick

Available next month
www.millsandboon.co.uk

COMING SOON!

We really hope you enjoyed reading this book. If you're looking for more romance, be sure to head to the shops when new books are available on

Thursday
18th October

LET'S TALK

Romance

For exclusive extracts, competitions
and special offers, find us online: